NEW RIVER SUMMERS

NEW RIVER SUMMERS

Jessie Shields Strickland

TATE PUBLISHING
AND ENTERPRISES, LLC

New River Summers
Copyright © 2012 by Jessie Shields Strickland. All rights reserved.

No part of this publication may be reproduced, stored in a retrieval system or transmitted in any way by any means, electronic, mechanical, photocopy, recording or otherwise without the prior permission of the author except as provided by USA copyright law.

Scripture quotations are taken from the *Holy Bible, King James Version,* Cambridge, 1769. Used by permission. All rights reserved.

This book is designed to provide accurate and authoritative information with regard to the subject matter covered. This information is given with the understanding that neither the author nor Tate Publishing, LLC is engaged in rendering legal, professional advice. Since the details of your situation are fact dependent, you should additionally seek the services of a competent professional.

The opinions expressed by the author are not necessarily those of Tate Publishing, LLC.

Published by Tate Publishing & Enterprises, LLC
127 E. Trade Center Terrace | Mustang, Oklahoma 73064 USA
1.888.361.9473 | www.tatepublishing.com

Tate Publishing is committed to excellence in the publishing industry. The company reflects the philosophy established by the founders, based on Psalm 68:11,
"The Lord gave the word and great was the company of those who published it."

Book design copyright © 2012 by Tate Publishing, LLC. All rights reserved.
Cover design by Joel Uber
Interior design by Nathan Harmony

Published in the United States of America

ISBN: 978-1-61862-667-7
1. Biography & Autobiography / Personal Memoirs
2. Family & Relationships / Love & Romance
12.02.28

Dedication

To you, Annie Ayers Reynolds, I dedicate *New River Summers*. Thank you for making my childhood special, your family mine, and your friendship perpetual. What a kind, inspiring role model you are. Thank you for being the mother of my first love, Dubs.

To you, Marion Gray Harkleroad, III, your nana loves every hair on your precious head, and I pass on my love for reading and writing to you. Always take care of your mama, my Jenna.

Acknowledgements

I acknowledge my family for their enduring kindness, especially my husband, Robert "Bob" Strickland, for patience and encouragement, and our daughter, Virginia "Jenna" Strickland Harkleroad, my biggest fan. Jenna enjoyed all the tales from the past, especially the first love one. Also, I thank my son-in-law, Marion, for giving us Caleb, Tristan, and Gray.

I acknowledge my Tennessee and Virginia family, friends, and acquaintances. Without them, I would have no stories to tell. They touched my life in many wonderful ways.

To my teachers from Valley Forge Elementary, Hampton High School, and East Tennessee State University who encouraged me from first grade through doctoral degree education. Without their diligence, caring, and skills, I would lack the confidence to write.

I acknowledge my only living sister, Sonya Shields Alexander, the baby of the family, for her unconditional love, optimism, and faith.

I hold in my heart my mother, Lena Virginia Pearman Shields, for being the greatest mother and encourager a child could have. I miss her every day. To my late sisters, Patricia Rose and Pamela Kay, and my late brother, Samuel "Sammy," you left us too soon; however, your kindness and love have never been forgotten.

I recognize the powerful aunts that were wonderful role models: Aunt Mary Umberger, Aunt Jessie Brooks, Aunt Helen Clark, Aunt Ada Bess Shields, Aunt Hazel Ikenberry, and Aunt Burnett Fox.

I acknowledge my cousin Bob Shields, my Uncle Nick, and Aunt Avis Shields's son for being a Tate-published author—buy his book.

I appreciate my precious sisters' children, Joshua, Isaiah, Amie, Lisa, Stephanie, Amanda, and Lauren, for their love and support; and Matthew, Conner, McKenna, Autumn, Ava, and Emme, my great-nephew and nieces.

I salute Tate Publishing for providing a venue for new authors.

Foreword

Jessie Shields Strickland, teacher, university professor, public school superintendent, and author, grew up in Appalachia. In *New River Summers,* Dr. Strickland gives us her story, a poignant, loving story of real life in and about this beautiful geographical area and its strong and caring people. Living in northeastern Tennessee and spending idyllic summers in New River, Virginia, she introduces us to her family and friends who make up, influence, and guide her life. As a very young girl she knew what was expected and tried to live up to it.

Jessie's love and admiration for her mother is always there. We get to know this strong, loving mother who was left to rear her five very young children alone at the sudden death of her husband, her decisions made and their consequences.

Sent to Virginia for the summers, Jessie found her first love with all its wonders and confusions, its joys, and heartaches. As the summers grew in number, we share in the maturing of this young girl.

New River Summers is a good read which will take you back and wrap you in the aura of life and living.
—E. Ruth Green, Ph.D., Author, The Dance of Life, Poetry of Living

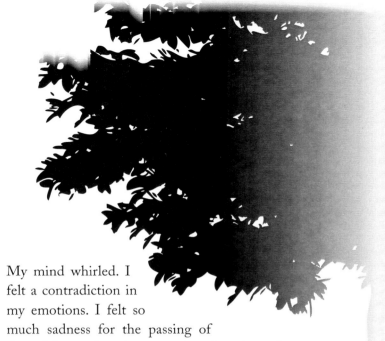

My mind whirled. I felt a contradiction in my emotions. I felt so much sadness for the passing of Aunt May, and at the same time, happiness in remembering an idyllic childhood in her care. I thought of the young, handsome boy who I had loved and left behind on the bank of the New River. For many summers I was enveloped in the giddiness and light heartedness of saying or writing his name…Dubs Jennings.

He was my first love this tall, tanned skin, sandy-blonde-haired and freckle- nosed boy with a fishing pole in hand. The vision was permanently etched in my mind's eye. I scribbled Jessica Jennings as a teenager so much I calloused my ring finger.

Dubs was a nickname I came to adore as I grew up traversing two states each summer to visit my beloved Aunt May and Uncle Art. I even thought of Dubs as I watched them lower her gunmetal-gray coffin into the cold Virginia earth. I had loved my aunt May like no other person on this earth. In this miserably freezing temperature, I felt wrapped in the warmth of all the happiness she had given me as a child. This was to be my only inheritance from her. It remains one of the best gifts I have ever received along with the memories of Dubs.

"Wake up, Ducky. Uncle will be here in an hour."

That had to be the sweetest words my mama could say each year at the beginning of summer. I felt suffocated in the northeastern Tennessee Appalachian Valley where I had been born and raised. My mama and daddy owned a small produce and poultry business. They knew this would be a good living in the Tennessee Valley to raise a family on. They meant to raise together five children; however, right after my fifth birthday in 1952, my Daddy died from a heart attack. His hard day of work was mostly lifting, loading, and hauling produce in his Ford truck from South Carolina to northeast Tennessee. *I had always felt as if I was stagnating in this town, but when Daddy died, we were really stuck. He had just come in, sat down* in his sun-streaked creased brown leather chair, asked Mama for an ash tray, and died. Her grief-stricken scream was heard above the cicadas and frogs for miles that evening. I can still hear it sixty-two years later.

Stuck. We were stuck for sure then. My mama and the five of us, Rose, 15, the oldest, Howard, 10, next, then the three of us under five, Kate, Jessica (that was me but nicknamed "Ducky" by my daddy from eight months old when I waddled like a duckling), and finally baby Helen. The River Doe snaking by our old weatherboard house with a wraparound porch would travel much farther than we ever would, I had thought at the time.

I guess you could say Mama's brother Emmett, from Roanoke, Virginia, and his biannual visits saved me from mountain confinement, dirt graveled roads, and bare feet that summer and all the summers to come for the next ten years. He made the annual trek to drop me off with my aunt and uncle in Austinville, Virginia.

I, Jessica "Ducky" Pearman, was the first of our family to venture outside the river valley. I knew my uncle was taking me because he felt sorry for us, especially Mama, who was left alone to rear five kids. I was glad I was considered a "happy child," "a no-trouble one," and "a peacemaker"; otherwise, he would have left me home with Mama along with her four other kids.

"She'll be no trouble on May," my uncle said to Mama.

He was right. I aimed to please my aunt May, Mama's younger sister, even though I did not know her or my uncle Art very well. I didn't know exactly where they lived, but I knew it was near the land where my mama had been born. She was given the name for that state, Virginia. I grew to love Virginia and named my only child after the state because of my childhood endearment to summer life there. After visiting my mama, Uncle Emmett passed close to my aunt and uncle's home on his return to Roanoke, Virginia, and deposited me like his old, worn suitcase.

Uncle stood on the gray porch with my paper-bag clothes carrier while I clung to mama's legs, bawling worse than baby Helen. I wanted to go, but I had never been away from my mama. I guess I felt a little guilty, too, leaving baby Helen. She was my favorite of them back then. Kate, only a year older, did not tolerate younger children.

I knew I'd return before school started, somewhere around Labor Day. I also knew no matter how sad leaving for the first time might be that I wouldn't miss the valley. No, siree, I would not miss the fish smell of the Doe, the dust, or the dirty feet with cuts from the graveled road. And I sure wouldn't miss hearing my mama crying into her pillow at night for my daddy.

Wrapping her arms around me at first sight was my aunt May. I couldn't help but notice I was almost as tall as she when her squeezing commenced.

"I'm going to fatten you up, child."

And she was true to her word. Aunt May and Uncle Art gave me the best welcome a Tennessee kid could ever have. I could not believe my luck.

She and Uncle Art, the local barber, had the best home place ever. Uncle Art's barber shop was the social center along the New River running by Austinville, Virginia. Austinville had been named by its founder Texan Stephen Austin, a statesman. The pleasant hamlet had once been a thriving lead mining resource but now had a paved street and two general stores in walking distance of the entrance and the exit of town. Even better, my aunt and uncle had a front porch with a row of caned rocking chairs with two large crab apple trees to shade them.

Aunt May could sew and did for the town people. Not only were all the men and boys coming for Uncle Art's shaves and haircuts, but I was getting to meet most of the women and girls coming for Aunt May's garment makings or sewing repairs. The ladies shared information (as they liked to call it) with Aunt May. Mrs. Jennings would start, "May, did you know Ella Jean Lantern had her baby? Don't say I said, but it came a little early."

"Law, law, May," eagerly retorted Mrs. King, "did you see where poor 'ole man Wright was in the paper under disorderly again?" And so went the information. The ladies would usually begin with a disclaimer such as, "May, just don't say I told you, but…" Then, the news about the families along the New River verbally flourished. I took my seat on the crushed wine-colored velveteen armed chair out of sight hanging on to every word. Aunt May would never respond but do an occasional shake of the head or mumble, "You don't say?"

Aunt May was a trooper. She was a good listener and a confidante. I was amazed at the tidbits of information the ladies would share—some got mighty personal. Aunt May would usually look at me, and the ladies took the hint that young ears were tuned in to the conversation. She never asked me to leave. As I think about that now, I must have been her excuse to halt the gossip or the personal dilemmas she was being told. The ladies would stop, ask Aunt May when their garment would be repaired, and leave.

My favorite playmate Dubs' mama often came to the sewing room. I liked her visits the most. She often spoke of Dubs and how much he was growing. This information made me feel older and wiser. Her visits were Aunt May's favorites, too. She talked about world news and the new walking trails being built across the river. No mindless chatter from Mrs. Jennings. She was a lady who was in touch with the world. She was full of facts and news worth hearing.

I never heard Aunt May repeat any information, good or bad, garnered from the sewing room. Her lips were stilled the moment the ladies left. She never told me to not repeat the information, because she knew that I would not. Aunt May and I had an unsaid agreement, what was said in the sewing room stayed in the sewing room. Aunt May was known for her listening skills and tight lips. The ladies needed someone to vent to, and Aunt May filled the bill. I learned a great deal from the ladies who frequented the sewing room. My greatest learning was from Aunt May. I learned from her example to keep my mouth shut and not carry tales. How could it get any better? It did. She cooked the best fried chicken, mashed potatoes, ham hock biscuits, and desserts, like putting homemade fudge and peanut butter between two saltine crackers. A kid could only dream about such "yumminess."

Uncle Art's and her two children were grown, married, and away. I was lucky on that, too. I felt loved the day I stepped on her wide porch. She wasn't normally a "warm fuzzy" person, but she made an exception when it came to me. I suppose she believed the rumor about my "peacemaker," "not much trouble," "happy child" reputation. And I was not going to let her down.

"Throw me the ball, Ducky!" said Pamela Stoots.

I did not know all I needed to know about the game of baseball, but I soon learned New River kids did. Right off,

I had to decide if I was a "Dodger" or a "Yankee." I took my cue from my freckle-faced, sandy-haired playmate named Edwin Wayne Jennings, known as "Dubs." Even though I was seven, I knew he was special. He would be my first love. He was a Yankee. From that day forward, I was a Yankee. Besides, the only true Dodger fan was the oldest girl in New River who played with us. Her name was Pamela, but we called her Pam, which sounded more like a girl ball player's name. She was plenty smart, real serious, and very large-framed. All of us younger kids seemed to get on her only nerve, her last one. We stayed out of her way and tried dodging her baseballs after she cracked a few bats in full swing with a force I had not seen from a girl. Perhaps "Dodger" would have been a more appropriate nickname for us rather than her.

I got better at baseball each summer. Dubs, Pam, her brother Clover, and her sister Sue Ann, saw to it. Sometimes Peter Lefpher, Jr. ("Junior" to us), and his younger brother, Saul, other New River baseball enthusiasts, neighbors, and playmates helped me with my swings or catches. Junior and Saul had a sister I adored, but she was always peeling potatoes and fixing supper for her working mom, dad, and ball-playing brothers. She was a faithful-to-the-task sister who was only a few years older than Junior but appeared relegated to that green linoleum-floored kitchen her whole childhood.

If it rained and the ball playing got cancelled, our crowd gathered on the Lefpher porch, exchanging tales and watching Marietta Lefpher peel those blasted potatoes. We should have been charitable enough to help her.

She never asked. And we never did. She just kept robotically peeling. Every now and then, she would chuckle at a tall tale coming from one of her brothers, which Dubs and I figured was a "crock of bull" tale.

For the most part, she respected our lazy days of summer, never complained, and turned out to be one heck of a cook, friend, mother, grandmother, and wife. I knew this: she had ample training on the cooking part. I knew another thing, too; our butts were off that porch well before the Lefpher parents ever drove into that gravel driveway in the blue Chevelle or red Chevy truck. These Lefpher Virginians were seriously Pentecostal and all business with their offspring.

I helped my aunt May any way I could just to get to the baseball field. Up the hill and out to the Stoot's cow pasture, I went.

Mostly, I took the grocery list and walked to Jenelle's store to get a loaf of Bunny bread, a can of ham shanks, and a pound of thickly sliced American cheese wrapped in white butcher paper, and an occasional cellophane package of sugared donuts. She threw in the donuts just for me. Uncle Art wouldn't touch 'em.

"Not homemade, May. I only eat homemade."

Lucky me.

I had the routine down. Get up at seven. Wash. Dress. Pray. Eat a full breakfast with the basic food groups covered twice: hot buttered biscuits, toast, country ham, bacon, fried eggs, stewed apples, and tomato slices.

Aunt May always described the food in each bowl or serving plate on the table. She made a quick introduction of the food which gave anticipation for each and every bite. To be at her table was an experience a child never forgot. I competed for one biscuit with four siblings in Tennessee, but Aunt May's daily spreads were bountiful. I could eat as many biscuits as polite without competition. I surely got my extra hefty appetite in life from Aunt May's tasty meals. The freshness and warmth of her breads, pies, and entrees were lip smacking and truly comforting. This part of our daily routine was my second favorite activity; staring at or sitting in close proximity to Dubs was my first.

We had the Stoot's dairy products—fresh cows milk every morning. Aunt May skimmed the rich cream off the top before she filled our glasses and saved the cream to make heavy whipped cream for her homemade chocolate or coconut cream pies for dinner meals, Uncle Art's favorites. That was one thing Uncle Art and I agreed upon.

Pam's family was in the dairy business. All the town people made trips to the Stoots's house just like they did to Aunt May and Uncle Art's house. New River people were hard workers and supported each other.

After breakfast, we cleared the table and washed the dishes. Aunt May still used a large metal pan in her sink, rather than use the sink itself, to wash the dishes. I dried them. She placed them back on the table to get ready for lunch. Instead of using hot water from the faucet, kettle-boiled scalding rinse water was poured over the dishes. She had this thing for "squeaky" clean.

Uncle Art went to the barber shop and worked steadily every day until noon, except Sunday. He would have worked then, but Aunt May was a Methodist woman of God and would not allow it. The Sabbath was coveted as a day of rest or for a truck ride to the Shot Tower, Fancy Gap, Cripple Creek, or Mabry Mill. Aunt May and I tidied bedrooms and then went to her dayroom. She sewed on the throttle-powered Singer while I idled on the daybed, looking through her baskets of kaleidoscopic colors in buttons and threads. In summers to come, she let me choose fabrics and patterns for new clothes. I always went home to Tennessee looking better than I came. She even gently turned me loose on the Singer, only to discover I was better at baseball than sewing.

She instinctively knew when Uncle Art was about to come to the porch even before the cuckoo had made its appearance in the living room from the antique clock. Lunch was set on a metal kitchen table. We took our places. We had our own distinct seating positions around the table.

Seating at the kitchen table did not vary for the ten New River summers in their home. Fried chicken or salmon croquettes, sweet pickle and mustard potato salad, garden peas dripping with Stoot's freshly churned cow's butter, and hot biscuits were common lunch fare.

As we ate and shared "people" stories, Uncle Art couldn't resist repeating the cleaner jokes he had been told by Herb down the road or the prank of Mr. Jackson's eldest up the road. Aunt May shared Mrs. Fisher's good news of her son's engagement or how many visitors she had that morning with sewing repairs.

I listened in awe. We had no dull moments at that table. I knew the New River people better than those in my Tennessee Valley home.

Uncle Art ate lunch and retreated to the front porch rocker until his next customer came. No appointments were made. Just walk-in service. First come, first served. No cash register either; it was just Uncle Art's khaki work pants' pockets for that. Change was kept in a Mason jar. Life was easy, intriguing, and kind on the New River. Time flowed peacefully and melodically like fog moving through the night after a soft summer rain.

I had only one lunch duty—to keep Uncle Art's company on the front porch. I performed my duty admirably. He didn't tolerate nonsense or chatter. He heard enough in the barber shop. Unlike Aunt May, he did like to talk about some of the more interesting customers, but not on the porch. The porch was his rest time, and the time he shared with me, just the two of us. My uncle and I understood the silent pact.

He drew a cherry smoking pipe from his pocket. He tapped it a couple times in his hand upside down, pulled a small, aging gauged-material tobacco pouch from his shirt pocket, filled the pipe right side up, and tapped the bow with his index finger. He struck a match on his shoe heel and settled into a place I did not know nor did he choose to tell me about. An unspoken covenant was upheld between the two of us when we were on the porch.

I sat as faithfully as any Coonhound dog. I took it all in, day after day, the crab apple trees, Uncle Art with his pipe, the waft of tobacco that blew in the breeze toward my rocker, the passersby who always waved but never stopped to talk, unless they wanted a shave or a cut.

They, too, knew this was Uncle Art's time. When the cuckoo sounded at 1:00 p.m., the spell was broken.

Uncle Art patted the top of my head and returned to the barber shop.

Just like clockwork, when Uncle left the porch, Aunt May appeared with the grocery list and cash, her sewing money. I walked down the street to Jenelle's or up the street to Jennings's grocery. It never mattered to me, because as soon as I returned from my daily duty, it was ballgame time in Stoot's field with the Dodgers and Yankees.

Every day we played unless the World Series hopefuls were in progress on TV. Then we sat cross-legged for hours in front of the Stoot's black and white 22" RCA screen. If Pam Stoot's Brooklyn Dodger baseball favorites Roger Maris, Sandy Koufax, Don Drysdale, and Willie Davis were playing, we were invited to watch in the Stoot's family room. Pam's parents were working at their dairy farm and had long hours. I had to walk down the hill after an hour to give Aunt May my whereabouts. I most always returned for at least another sixty minutes.

Out of the three Stoot's children, Pam was the boss, or should I say bossiest? Pam said it; we did it, except when it came to turning us into Dodger fans. We rebelled, but we didn't brag about it, at least not in front of Pam. Dubs, Peter, Junior (a sacrificial Dodger who had to be called Dodger in name only), Saul, Sue Ann, Clover (another sacrificial Dodger), and I became New York Yankees to the bone, secretly rooting for Mickey Mantle, Gene Woodling, Billy Martin, Whitey Ford, and Joe Collins. Pam was never the same after Mickey won the Triple Crown. Even the sacrificial Dodgers. To have a team could not contain their happiness. The Yankees showed Pam Stoots.

Time flew by, and before I knew it, Uncle Emmett came from Roanoke to get me. My heart ached. I would almost make myself sick thinking about leaving the security of Aunt May and Uncle Art's home and my Yankees and Dodgers New River friends, especially Dubs. He grew on me over the years. I even missed Pam and her sweet sister, Sue Ann, who had a Southern elegance even while she did the milking and churning

Each summer I traveled back to Tennessee with Uncle Emmett to return to school. Mama didn't drive; however, she tried once, after she tore the nose off my aunt Miranda's green and white Nash. Aunt Miranda's husband, my favorite uncle who went by the moniker "Jug," lucked out and won that Nash from holding his lucky number from the carnival. Mama was forbidden behind the wheel after that. Also, the only gated estate we had in our River Doe area, called *Journey's End*, ironically became Mama's end to any hopes of automobile independency. She took the sign part that said "End" down with the nose of the Nash.

Uncle Emmett always wore a suit with a diamond tie tack on his tie, a hat tilted to the side, black-and-white-toed wing-tipped leather shoes, and Old Spice cologne. He was not married during my trips to Virginia, even though he had been three times in his earlier years. He was a car salesman. I never knew which kind of car we would be traveling in. I didn't care. It only added to my uncle's mystique along with the Old Spice.

Mama said he always had a nice female to see to his needs, even if I didn't see her. It was a good thing, too, because he was very tight with his money. Our solo stop for ten years traveling Interstate 81 after several hours was always the same—a Virginia rest area right before the Tennessee line. Our one snack was always the same—cold water from the rest area fountain. He dressed like a million dollars, but he never spent a dime on me or him at that rest stop. I could have used a grape Nehi or any soda pop back then; however, I was grateful to my uncle for reliability, storytelling, and consistency. Somehow I felt comforted in the sameness of our routine. I knew Uncle Emmett was taking me to my favorite home away from home. Interstate 81, in its familiarity, took me to a place of safety and happiness. My uncle left nothing to the imagination. I knew him well and looked forward to our time together and his unwavering dependability. I counted on him to come get me and take me to Aunt May's each summer. He never disappointed me.

"What did you do, Ducky, at Aunt May's and Uncle Art's?" Voices rang out in unison from my siblings the moment I got home. I never told them much. I could see Mama's face and those large doe eyes of hers and couldn't bear to let her know I had enjoyed my summers on the New River more than I did the home she had made for us- a widowed mother bringing up five children on her own the very best she could.

 I didn't want to tell anyone in Tennessee about my special summers for fear those magical times would be erased. I held onto those summer days through all the harsh winters. My thoughts sustained me until I again returned to the crab apple-shaded front porch, the smell of Uncle Art's sweet cherry-scented tobacco, and to my New River friends, especially Dubs.

Mama would take me in her welcoming embrace. She was a large-framed woman, much taller than Aunt May. Her strength was felt in those embraces. My mama was an educated woman, finishing at East Tennessee State Normal School, now East Tennessee State University. She had taught in one-room schoolhouses in Roan Mountain and Cove Creek and had boarded with a family who would take a teacher, such as herself, in to their mountain home to subsidize their meager incomes.

She met my dad on a hayride after her poppa, my grandfather, moved to Tennessee in the early '30s. They mutually agreed they weren't getting any younger and that they should marry. The wedding was a justice of the peace affair. "Short and sweet" my mama called it. My mama and her two younger sisters had been on their own for sixteen years. Mama often reminisced about her mama who died at age forty coming home from Wednesday night church. My grandmother Laura was walking behind her children down the lane to their farmhouse. When she failed to come home shortly behind the children, my grandfather knew something was amiss. He took the buggy to look for her and found her crumpled body resting eternally beneath an oak tree that shaded the lane.

My grandfather was in a pickle—five children and no one to mother them. Shortly thereafter, he remarried. The stepmother was not keen on having a brood of children in the farmhouse with her. Two of the children, my Uncle

Emmett and Aunt May, were old enough to move out on their own and made a life for themselves. My mama and the two younger sisters were put in a house close by on the property. Since my mama was the oldest at nine, she took charge. She said my grandfather, the post master and general store owner, came every day to check on them; the stepmother did not come. My mama never had much to tell us about my grandfather's wife. She only referred to her as Ms. Lilly.

My mama put herself through college and saw to it my aunts did well, too. She was a child raising children, but she did the best she could do. My grandfather was a good provider of necessities. As peculiar as the divided family seemed, they made it work. Better being in a separate house than being in the house where Ms. Lilly resided. Mama and her two sisters were bonded for their lifetime. They attended each others' weddings. They rejoiced together; they wept together.

My aunts were pleased to see my mama happy and marrying my daddy made her so. They were the same age, 28, when they married. Daddy's family, especially my granddaddy, who was a country doctor, was relieved to see him get a good-educated woman like my mama. She loved his family as much as she did him. My mama had lived a lifetime to most before she was 28 years old, so marrying my daddy seemed a natural progression in her life and a joy. She loved my daddy the nineteen years she had him, but life seemed to play horrible tricks on my mama. Loving and losing seemed a common thread in her wise life. In the late '30s, you couldn't teach if you were married. The mountain communities set this as a standard. The board of education or district administrator enforced it. Pregnancy was next to a curse. Married women teachers would have been risky business. A married woman might get pregnant; this would be unseemly and disgraceful to be pregnant and teach. However, the rules of marriage did not apply to men teachers.

My mama loved her teaching years and spoke of them often, recounting events that occurred in the one room school house. She taught the basic curriculum of reading, writing, and arithmetic and boarded with a man and his wife near the school she was assigned in the mountains. Her career choice was teaching or daddy. Mama chose daddy. Her own five children replaced the children she loved and missed from the classroom.

Daddy proved a challenge to mama. No wonder my granddaddy was so thrilled to have my mama with daddy. My brother and sisters soon knew why. My daddy loved not only my mama but a hefty bottle of sipping whiskey. Our family never lacked for anything like so many other families along the Appalachians. He ran a fresh produce and poultry business with a small diner so Mama never had to worry about feeding us. He overindulged with that darn sipping whiskey my first four years of life, then sobering the fifth year only to meet the Grim Reaper at the age of forty-seven. Mama remembered him as "perfect"—funny how death and time erased his flawed traits.

My parents' marriage was a no-frills relationship, but nevertheless, they married. My mama was a late bloomer, too. She had me at the age of forty and bore baby sister

Helen at forty-two. Mama was always the oldest mother at our school. She became the most beloved because of her humor, kindness, fairness, and pancakes. Our old house was inviting to all our playmates, especially the hungry ones.

Our table was open to all who came across her porch. Sharing was always the only option with my mama. I guess that figured into the equation of why I liked Aunt May and Uncle Art so well. I was their main interest, no sharing with anyone but me for five weeks and three days, give or take a few days, every summer. Yes siree, what kid wouldn't have liked all that Virginia love, new clothes, a secret love, and peanut butter fudge crackers to herself?

"What happened to all your hair?" I said. I noticed on one return New River trip that baby Helen, now ten, and Sister Kate, thirteen, had traded their long chestnut-colored braids, for short, bobbed haircuts. Rose and Howard were snickering. Their hair was pretty much the same. If I had not known better, I would have sworn Uncle Art had gotten hold of Helen and Kate with one of his no-nonsense haircuts—the "special" ten-cent one.

They shrugged. They remained speechless until Uncle Emmett left the front yard and was out of hearing distance. Mama began, "Well, it is a good thing you went to Aunt May's this summer! We have new neighbors. They have moved into the old Borland house with eleven children. Ducky, the two youngest Borland girls came over to play with Helen and Kate. Those were the hungriest kids, so I fed them at the table. Helen and Kate's heads started itching a few days later."

She didn't have to say another word—eek, head lice! I could not believe my ears. I knew this was a social dilemma for Mama and even more reason to leave this place in the summer for me. I knew kids who had it but never us.

Mama was vigilant. She performed daily "nit" head checks after each school day. The "nit-picking" along with the tar-smelling head and hair scrub was applied daily for seven days. Every item of bedding, brushes, combs, and furniture was cleaned as well for seven days. She had gotten lax too soon. When summer came, she thought her "nit" worries were over. The "lousy" kids, as they were called, were home for the summer. She had not expected the new neighbors to harbor the most dreaded contagion to mountain kids—lice.

She never dreamed summer would wreck such havoc. To catch head lice was no shame, but to keep it was. I spent the next thirty minutes listening to Helen and Kate's descriptions of purging this pestilence from heads and home. I always heard good comes from bad. In this case, it did. Mama made a sharing decision in our favor. She would still feed the Borland kids just like the other dozen or so from the valley in the summer, but she would do it outside in the backyard, picnic-style. The plan worked well, especially for Helen and Kate. We never had to worry about lice again in the house, and the Borlands as well as the neighborhood kids, got fed.

Kids didn't always go to school to get an education in the Appalachian Mountains in the '50s. Many went to eat. The cooks could give second servings. Kids couldn't get enough government commodity pinto beans, macaroni and cheese, and peanut butter cookies. The aroma of freshly baked yeast rolls beckoned the kids, me included, to the lunch line like a gambler to a lottery. The "seconds" bowls displayed in front of the glassed-in cooks' station were scraped clean daily.

The teachers gave 100-percent awards for a clean plate. I came home every day almost light-headed that I had earned a 100 percent. This went on for weeks. My mother thought I was a prodigy until she discovered on parent-teacher conference day my 100's were coming from clean plates rather than scores on my classroom subjects. I attributed my voracious appetite to this day to my "clean plate" daily challenges. I am sure my summer visits to Aunt May's helped develop my appetite.

"Uncle Emmett, how much longer before we get there?" My anticipation to arrive in New River grew with each summer's passing. I had turned twelve in November and had my first monthly. I thought it was the chocolate milk I had drunk from breakfast, and that it had passed from my throat to my undies. I felt more grown up after Mama had given me "the talk."

I could have been just as happy with a book about it. Her stern face had this written all over it: "You are a woman now, Ducky. You need to conduct yourself like one." I didn't know quite what to think about being a woman if it meant I couldn't be a Yankee anymore.

Mama made me walk to the country store with a note to get sanitary pads. I hoped Mrs. Taylor, the grocer's wife, would be the recipient of my mama's penciled note written on the corner of a torn paper bag. It was not to be. Her husband, Cliff, was.

A girl of twelve can just look so long through an oak display cabinet of combs, bobby pins, Jo-Curl, permanent solutions, and hair nets. I ambled about the store pretending to look at the limited merchandise, but I actually was trying to scope the store for Mrs. Taylor. All I saw was five old men gathered around the Buckeye coal stove discussing the *Farmer's Almanac* planting section and looking annoyed as Cliff was being taken from the discussion by a twelve year old who was taking her sweet time looking at "junk." I didn't think they could tell I was a woman. They sure didn't act any differently, and for that I was mighty thankful.

I could no longer deny the inevitable. After Cliff's fifth time to the counter, he said, "Ducky, can I help you or not?"

I slipped him the note as covertly as I could. He read it and nodded as if he understood the issue that held me hostage to my own paralysis. On the note was Mama's scrawling: "One box of Kotex for Jessica. Please charge to my account." She had signed it: "Lydia Pearman."

I had not read the note until Cliff did. I couldn't believe she used my birth name—talk about a traitor. If she hadn't felt the need to tell the world about my monthly, I could have acted like the pads were for Kate or Rose. Helen was too young. Her biggest worry was missing an episode of Dale Evans and Roy Rogers on the 19" black and white. Rose never discussed her personal life. Never. I didn't think Kate had a personal life other than books and art. Plotting and writing her fantasy trips to Milan and Florence were her worries and passions. Knowing Kate, she wouldn't have cared if she had to hand Cliff the note. She might have made him blush.

Not to worry. Cliff moved toward the very back of the store beyond the snack-and-yak fellowship that was leaning their chairs with feet resting on the oil-coated plank floors.

I was saved, so I thought, until Cliff shook a large brown bag with his polio-inflicted bent hand and yelled, "Ducky, do you want 'ragular' or large?"

Every eye in the store was on me. Scarlet-faced, I managed to barely squeak: "The little ones, please, Mr. Taylor." Who knew being a woman came in different sizes? Mama hadn't bothered to fill me in on that part.

Needless to say, every old coot who hung out at the store knew I was "a woman" now…geez.

Getting to New River this year would be a welcomed relief from my entry into womanhood. Mama at least had the common decency to stock up on pads for me to take on the annual maneuver from the valley.

I was not intending to tell Aunt May about it, either. But they knew. I could tell it the moment Aunt May grabbed me, and the first words from her mouth were, "Well, well, little Jessica, you have grown up since the last time we saw you."

Like I hadn't noticed with the use of my birth name… this womanhood thing was serious business with old people.

What in the Sam Hill did that mean? My mama had blabbed about my being a woman? Did my mama have no shame? I wouldn't have been surprised if the deep voice of Mr. WBED himself, the local radio voice of town celebrity and decorated war hero Mason Morris, would announce my dismal state on the seven o'clock news.

Unpacking was quick, but I had to wait out lunch. I wasn't hungry. I was too excited to see my New River friends, especially Dubs, to wait and eat. I was losing daylight.

Uncle Emmett left late afternoon, making it too late to join the Dodgers and Yankees. I suddenly panicked. What if Pam and Sue Ann had become women during the winter? Would these change things for us? Surely Pam was a woman by now. She was three years older than I and four years older than Sue Ann. She still played ball with us. Maybe this woman thing wasn't so bad after all.

No sooner had that thought entered my mind when I saw what appeared to be Dubs, fishing pole in hand, wearing a blue oxford shirt hanging over khaki shorts, coming down the hill from his house. He was heading toward Uncle Art's barbershop, it appeared, to fish in the New River.

Another good thing about Uncle Art's house was that it faced the Jennings' house. Before this day, I had seen Dubs as a favorite playmate, good pitcher, and ultimate Yankee fan.

I saw Dubs as cute, but something had happened. He was fourteen this summer. Now, I saw him as almost godlike.

As he came closer to the porch, I found it hard to speak. His sandy-colored hair was more sun streaked. His freckled face more tanned and defined. His green eyes more sparkling and pronounced. All the baseball playing and exercise, with another year's age, had made for muscled arms and legs. He was taller—much taller.

I hadn't noticed any of this before. What was happening to me? I didn't know, but I liked the way it felt. Maybe that woman thing had kicked in the first pleasantness I had encountered from it.

Dubs spoke to Uncle Art first, then Aunt May. Aunt May asked about his mama, Sarah. She was the postmaster and well liked with a sterling reputation. She had the same kind demeanor as my mama—the neighborhood favorite of all the kids, too.

That summer would turn out to be one of my best. Dub's mama and Aunt May saw to it. Dubs Jennings peered directly at me. "You want to go fishing, Ducky?"

Boy, did I! Did he say fishing? I had never gotten that excited over baiting hooks with slimy earthworms before, so all doubt vanished about the monthly not changing me into a woman. With that cycle came a different attitude about the opposite sex. Last summer, Dubs was a playmate and a fellow pretend Yankee; now a year later, he was a larger-than-life major crush. I was smitten with rapid heart palpitations, sweaty palms, and jumbled thoughts. Everything Mama made me read from the public library in the girls-to-women book was true. At the time, I resented it, embarrassed by the contents of it. But it was true, revealed by a firsthand, honest-to-goodness experience right there on the banks of the New River.

Jessie Shields Strickland

I knew that whether or not I went fishing with Dubs was going to be Uncle Art and Aunt May's decision. It was a good thing, too, because for the first time in my twelve years, I was speechless. Southern girls know that to answer a boy's invitation too enthusiastically or to not yield to the adults for an answer could be the kiss of death, and my uncle and aunt may not let me go. I just hesitated, looking as neutral as I could considering the raging hormonal activity inside me, and gave my uncle and aunt time to answer for me.

Uncle Art looked at Aunt May. The answer passed silently between them. I never heard a word, but Aunt May said, "Ducky, don't be long. Dinner will be ready at five."

Off the porch, I went. "Thank you, Aunt May and Uncle Art. I'll be back at five." I made sure I gave my most appreciative response and remained calm, even though my heart was thumping in my ears.

I didn't have a pole. I hadn't changed from my traveling clothes. But I truly wanted to go fish with a boy who now appeared much older and wiser. Life was getting even better on the New River.

"I saw your uncle pull in the driveway, saw him from the living room window," Dubs remarked smugly.

"You did?" This was all I could think to say as my heart raced and my brain fogged.

"Uh-huh, Ducky, and your aunt May told Mother you would be here today. I was going fishing earlier but decided to wait. You like to fish?"

I was about as good at fishing as I was at baseball, but I managed to retort, "Pretty good, but I always fish with yellow corn." The brain fog temporarily lifted, so I wouldn't later have to bait a hook with an earthworm and pass out.

We were on the grassy knoll of the New River. I guess this was kind of like my first "woman" outing with a guy.

Dubs Jennings was leaning against the large, smooth-barked trunk of a sprawling weeping willow. He had one foot kicked back on the trunk for support as well as masculine appeal, while he baited the hook with an earthworm. I looked away to survey find a place to perch and found a soft green spot. I sat down as womanly as possible. I could hear my mama's words: "Ducky, you are a woman now; conduct yourself like one."

I watched Dubs, who was taking his fishing mighty seriously. I thought he looked even better, now than when he came down the hill from his house, if that was possible.

The scattered midafternoon sun rays streaked through the willow limbs and cut slanted patterns around him. I could look at him all I wanted, if I didn't go blind first from the sunlight, and he would just keep on fishing. He had an angled jawline, perfect white teeth, and a crooked grin. His eyelashes were long and curled a bit over his deep set, penetrating green eyes. At that very moment, I did not see one iota of imperfection. From my seated position, backed by only the sounds from natural elements surrounding us, he appeared almost mythical, a Thor type, framed by the intensity of a pale blue sky and an occasional drifting cloud.

Geez, I had a knotted stomach from the thoughts of him, but the most euphoric state settled over my twelve-year-old frame. I could have sat on that riverbank looking up at Dubs until Uncle Emmett came for me to head back to Tennessee. This one memory became inscribed in my mind permanently, even after sixty-two years.

The exact moment first love occurs cannot be timed or foretold. No preparation is necessary. No one can explain the emotion unless one has experienced it. The very sweetness of it evades all senses. If the feelings are innocently reciprocated, the memory is etched forever. The sight of Dubs enveloped me. My mind's eye photographed him; I observed him with the greatest of concentration. I generously stared, not exactly what a Southern lady-in-training should necessarily do, but that's exactly what I did, until Uncle Art's deep voice messed the whole picture up with, "Catching anything, Dubs?"

"No, sir, not today. They aren't biting," Dubs answered.

They continued men's talk. I eventually got up as womanlike as possible, and said, "Good-bye, Dubs, and I guess you can start calling me 'Jessica' this summer. After all, it is my real name," and walked without Uncle Art back to the yellow clapboard house.

Aunt May was beside herself. She must have been cooking straight through from my last trip. She had enough food to feed Sherman's troops. And all I could think about was Dubs and the way the sunlight had captured his lovely face in its rays.

Becoming a woman had affected me more than I realized. All those tangled-up emotions were trickling over me like a babbling brook.

I liked the warm feeling I got when I saw or thought about Dubs. I liked knowing I could see him weeks on end. I liked knowing he was on the hill overlooking my aunt May's house. I liked knowing he seemed to return my most private of feelings.

Dubs returned those feelings in supporting me at the baseball field in the Stoots' pasture. He stood closer to me and would occasionally pat my shoulder in a silent commendation of my baseball skills as a Yankee. Shucks, I didn't think I was all that great, but that pat on the shoulder was all the motivation I needed to keep me returning to the ball field daily.

He walked down the hill more frequently, and as he did, he seemed to always throw a sideways glance at Uncle Art's front porch. He confided to me that he turned down a scouting weekend trip because he could scout when I wasn't at the New River.

A glance, a smile, a nod of approval were other small ways Dubs let me know he felt special about me. Geez, I think first love was even better that Aunt May's fudge and peanut butter crackers. I knew I had matured in ways of the heart. Last summer, I would have chosen the crackers every time.

I recalled a quote I had read once from the holy saint herself, Mother Teresa. I believed her now as I pondered on her words: "Love is a fruit always in season."

I knew Dubs was my first love. Edwin Wayne "Dubs" Jennings was the "fruit always in season," especially during a lazy summertime for an adolescent girl from the Tennessee Valley, whose lingering thoughts of him have lasted almost a lifetime.

I had never dreamed about much in my life that I could remember other than the reoccurring dream of hanging onto a grapevine for dear life, afraid to turn loose for fear a black bear from the Smokey Mountains would get me. I had seen a bear at a family reunion. I never forgot it. The dream was so real that I would wake up tired, with aching arms. This night I dreamed without fear or the bear.

In Aunt May's and Uncle Art's home, I felt safe and happy. As I drifted off, a gentle breeze blew through the open window screen, enticing with the sweet smell of lilac from Aunt May's garden into the bedroom. I saw Dubs against the willow in my mind's eye as I sunk deeply into the goose down pillow and soft mattress. He was beautiful, more beautiful than Troy Donahue, Tommy Sands, or Frankie Avalon, my celebrity crushes.

"Ducky, would you like to go to Hungry Mother State Park today with Mrs. Jennings, Rachel Ann, Dubs' baby sister Sissy, Dubs, and Junior?"

Was I still dreaming? No, I wasn't. Aunt May repeated it as I opened my eyes.

"Yes, yes, I would, Aunt May."

"Can you swim, Ducky?" Aunt May asked.

"Yes, I can swim well."

This was the absolute truth. I was a fair baseball player, a fair fisherwoman, but if I could do anything well, it was swim. The River Doe, the Hammond public swimming pool, and the nearby Johnson City Munsey Memorial

Methodist Church indoor swimming pool, made me a better than average swimmer.

What a way to start a Monday! No school, no helping Mama fix peanut-butter-and-jelly sandwiches for the neighborhood Pughette and Borland kids, and no fussing with grumpy older sister Kate. I wondered, *were we too old to play Dodgers and Yankees?* It didn't seem as important now as it once had. I was going to Hungry Mother State Park.

"Aunt May, where is this Hungry Mother State Park?" I had remembered seeing the exit sign on I-81 many times as Aunt May's answered my question. "Are you going with us, Aunt May?"

"Gracious, no, Ducky, he," she said, nodding her head toward the barbershop vicinity, "can't do without me." When I thought back, I could never remember a time they were apart.

Somehow, I believed her.

She went on, "Hungry Mother State Park is in Marion, Virginia, and gets it name from a legend about a woman who had been hurt but escaped her Indian captives with a small child. The legend has it that along a creek bank in Smyth County, Virginia, white men found her body, with the child alive and crying, 'Hungry, mammy.' Now, what do you say to that, Ducky? Still want to go?"

"Yes, of course, Aunt May." It sounded like a spooky place, but how bad could it be with Dubs there? Wild horses or a spooky story could not have held me back from the trip to Hungry Mother Park.

"Well, then, it's settled. Here, put your swimsuit in this." Aunt May was beaming. She held a royal blue, marigold yellow, and red-striped beach towel and a large woven straw bag with three red straw flowers sewn onto the side.

"Oh, thank you, Aunt May. I love them both." She must have conspired with Mrs. Jennings to have been so prepared. She must have sacrificed a week's worth of sewing money for me. My heart overflowed with love for this kind and generous relative who was like a second mother.

I barely managed to contain myself at the breakfast table. I force-fed myself, mostly moving food around on my plate to make it look like I had eaten so as not to disappoint Aunt May. I ate my fried egg, drank the Stoot's milk, and decided that was enough nourishment, and Aunt May's feelings would remain intact.

Before we could do the dishes, Uncle Art had the first customer of the week for a cut and shave. Soon to follow, Aunt May had Mrs. Porter at the door for a hemming job. I cleared the table, washed the dishes, put them back on the table for lunch, and headed for the shower house.

I had become a permanent fixture around Aunt May's home. Everything came naturally in the reoccurrence of events. There is something to be said for consistency. I never did believe it was the "hobgoblin of little minds," as I had read from my eighth grade English lit book. Consistency in my life had done me more good than harm.

When 10:00 a.m. arrived, and Mrs. Jennings drove off the hill, Aunt May and I moved to the familiar front porch. She put a dollar bill in my beach bag, gave me a hug, and waved me off. I moved into the Plymouth Valiant's backseat and smiled as I nodded to Mrs. Jennings Dubs, Junior, and Dubs's older sister, Rachel Ann, eighteen, and

Sissy, six. Getting into that Valiant was one of the best experiences of my life in the summers. I felt welcomed and loved by the Jennings' family.

I loved my aunt May, too. That morning she endeared herself to me. The dollar bill she placed in my beach bag was the very dollar I had seen Mrs. Porter give her for the hemming. Was there no end to her unselfishness and kindness?

Surveying the sandy man-made beach at Hungry Mother Park as Mrs. Jennings stopped the car, Dubs asked, "What do you think of this place, Ducky? Isn't it a beauty?"

"Indeed it is, Dubs," I answered dreamily. "Indeed it is."

The surrounding mountains stood stunningly above the dark green lake waters that enveloped 108 acres of beauty. Mrs. Jennings told us the park had been built in the 1930's and was one of six built in Virginia by the Civilian Conservation Corps, or CCC.

Then I spotted it. I couldn't believe my luck. About a third of the way across the lake was a large wooden platform with diving boards at two different elevations. I pictured my pike dive from the higher board. I forgot all the "conduct yourself like a woman" Mama talk when it came to swimming. I could hang right in there with the boys. I was looking forward to a little friendly competition.

Mrs. Jennings, Rachel Ann, Sissy, and I made our way to the bathhouse on the left. Dubs and Junior veered to the bathhouse on the right.

I was thanking my lucky stars as I pulled my new red Lycra knit swimsuit from the straw bag. My aunt Miranda, mama's sister and former driver trainer, had bought my siblings and me each a swimsuit before school ended for the summer break. This would be the first time I had worn my new red swimsuit.

As I pulled it on and up, I noticed it had this cupped bra-like thing in the top. I didn't give it much thought at the time, just thinking it was a clever addition. Perhaps I should have. It was my first swimsuit with a built-in bra. Vanity made me think I would look better at the top with such a built-in addition. *"Humility always followed vanity,"* echoed in my ears from Mama. I should have heeded her words, as I was about to discover.

Mrs. Jennings had already claimed our spot, spread the beach towels, set up the picnic basket, and deposited the Coppertone suntan lotion bottle in the hot sand.

Could this be a more perfect day? was my thought. The only thing that would have been better was for Aunt May and Uncle Art to have been there or Mama and my brother and sisters. They weren't; I was. The guilt was a fleeting thought. It evaporated into the clear blue sky as Dubs, Junior, and I ran for the cold, dark lake water.

"Yikes!" yelled Dubs. The lake water had not warmed enough from the colder than normal southwestern Virginia winter. Mrs. Jennings, Rachel Ann, and Sissy had figured out the water temperature by our squeals and stayed lodged on the towel retreat. I was so used to swimming in the River Doe in early spring that I plunged headfirst into the cold water along with Dubs and Junior, who followed me at a rapid pace.

We swam our way to the anchored diving platform, climbed the ladder, and jumped repeatedly from the diving boards. I decided to put a hold on my diving exhibition until later or at least until after the boys dived. I needed to evaluate my competition. We continued to follow the leader, taking turns with can openers, cannon balls, twists, flips, and jumps until we saw Mrs. Jennings waving us in for lunch. By that time, the water and high speed activity famished. Stopping for a refuel was no problem.

Rachel Ann was soaking up the rays and creating quite a stir with the boys from nearby Emery and Henry College. What was wrong with college boys and girls? Couldn't they see how much more fun swimming was than sitting around gawking at each other, listening to music on their transistor radios, or throwing a football?

As we dried ourselves with spare towels, Dubs looked over at me. He had that same snug look I had seen when we were on the New River fishing bank, but this time he added a lazy wink. Geez, maybe I had it all wrong. There is something to be said about gawking at each other if the right person's gawking at you. I quickly reassessed my "gawking" stance and decided not to be so narrow-minded about college kids and their priorities at Hungry Mother Park that day.

The chicken salad sandwiches and chips were washed down with Mrs. Jennings' pink lemonade. We leaned back on our towels to let our food digest. Mrs. Jennings was a firm believer in staying out of the water thirty minutes after eating to prevent muscle cramps. I didn't want to drown, so I gladly followed her advice. Besides, I needed to work my plan mentally for my pike dive. I could throw in a jackknife and a back dive, perhaps. The boys kicked sand, whispered, and joked around. Sissy made use of her yellow sand bucket and shovel.

After our thirty-minute digestion lag, Mrs. Jennings released us to the lake like freshwater trout. This time Rachel Ann with her shoulder-length, shiny brown hair moved her perfectly shaped silhouette with us. As she moved toward us, half the college boys on the beach moved toward Rachel Ann. Rachel Ann was surrounded in no time, and a beach ball ascended from the "frat pack." Rachel Ann, with her magnetic personality and unwavering manicured look, joined the frats and sorority sisters, monopolizing the male attention as the best-looking chick on the beach. Mrs. Jennings never took her laser focus from those of us in the water, Sissy in the sand, or the college boys around Rachel Ann. Mrs. Jennings maneuvered like a periscope.

Of course this left Dubs, Junior, and me to swim back to the platform unencumbered by others. I thought surely Dubs and Junior would dive this round; however, they did not.

We continued with our jumping antics and then sat on the platform facing away from Mrs. Jennings's line of vision. We kicked our feet back and forth in the water and watched the park guests enjoy rides up and down the lake in manual-powered paddle boats. We exchanged ideas for other summer activities. Since neither Dubs and Junior were old enough for a driver's license, we were totally dependent on others, like Rachel Ann or Mrs. Jennings, to provide wheels for our ideas. We were at their mercy.

As ideas like a community dance, a movie getaway, and a church picnic followed, Dubs casually took his hand and slid it over mine. My heart's rapid beating returned with his first touch to my skin. Does it get any better than this? I could not imagine beyond this moment—sitting on a platform in the middle of the lake, Dub's hand over mine. Tiny goose bumps formed over my skin. For the first time, I knew Dubs liked me more than as a ballplayer. I had hoped for this moment. Confirmation was in his eyes as I met them with mine.

For several minutes, we let Junior give us his best fishing tale, his baseball standouts in the Big League, and his brief knowledge of New River gossip—all uncontested by us. I didn't take in many of the details. It was the most conversation I had ever heard from Junior, and it was one-way. Junior didn't seem to notice. He was the focus of our attention, or so he thought.

Who were Dubs and I to spoil his moment? We sure didn't want him spoiling ours.

Then, we heard Rachel Ann behind us. Dubs and I stood up, but Dubs never dropped my hand. No one seemed to notice but me as he led me to the diving area.

Dubs, Jr., Rachel Ann, and I headed for the diving boards at the lowest elevation to begin our follow-the-leader antics. Rachel Ann went off first. She dived decently. When you looked like Rachel Ann, no one cared if you could swim, much less dive. Then Junior did a belly buster that left him chili-pepper red from his throat to his kneecaps. We laughed. Junior even laughed—all he could do after such an embarrassing belly flopper. He was a great sport even if he acted maimed the rest of the day. Dubs did a very decent dive. I certainly thought his good looks made up for any shortcomings in his dives. Then I was on the board—show time!

We had garnered the attention of the land lovers. All eyes were on me. I breathed deeply and walked to the center of the diving board. Pacing myself one, two, and on three, I went up at the very end of the board, then bent down, putting weight into the spring of both feet, which pivoted me high enough to tuck and touch my toes with a perfectly arched back. I released with toes pointing, head down, and legs as straight as an arrow, and sliced vertically into the wet stillness. I knew it was my best jackknife dive ever the moment my fingertips sensed the cold liquid. This moment was clearly the vanity part my mama had given reference all her life. I just had not registered it as a truism that humility would soon follow.

I surfaced to rousing handclaps and cheers of "Way to go, Ducky" from my friends and could hear the same echoing handclaps from the white sandy beach. I surveyed Dubs's face and smile for approval. The dive earned me another wink, making my day's anxiety of diving worth it. Then Dubs dived again. Good, not great, but an admirable job.

Rachel Ann had already climbed to the next challenge—the higher elevated diving board. She stood on the end of the board, dived, and entered the water with legs together and toes pointed—not bad. She received thunderous applause and roaring hoots with cat-calling whistles from the beach. It wasn't that good a dive, but she had mustered an entire cheering section with it anyway.

Poor Junior actually climbed the ladder next with a limp from his previous fiasco. His spirit had not been dampened by the belly flop. Even though he retained some of the red streaks from his first dive, he was not deterred. He, too, went to the end of the board. He fell toward the water like tumbleweed from the Mojave Desert, almost flip-flopping on his back and narrowly escaping a back-buster this time. Junior surfaced to cheers, not so much for his dive, but for his bravery. That boy needed to stick to New River baseball before he seriously injured himself.

I had already decided the forward pike was my dive of choice. I tested the spring from the higher altitude. I back-stepped to the center, ran through my mind what my swimming coach taught me, counted as I moved forward and, springing as high as I could go, ascended into the air like an eagle, rotating my body as I descended with a one-and-one-half somersault in a pike position, entering the lake headfirst. I felt the force of the water thrust against my chest. I surfaced.

Spectators from the beach were on their feet whistling and cheering. I had a diving ovation. Vanity consumed me. I quickly noticed my friends on the platform did not bask in my glory as I had expected. Immediately Dubs came off the board feet-first and almost landed on top of me.

What the heck was that about? What was he doing? I nearly choked to death with the unexpected gulp of lake water I drank as it swept over me from the wake he had created.

"Dubs? What are you doing? You nearly drowned me!"

With lightning speed, he cried out, "Ducky, your bathing suit has come apart at the top!"

As I quickly looked down to check out the condition of my hot red Janzen Lycra swimsuit causing my friend's discontent, I immediately saw the problem. Sure enough, humility was about to confront me. The force of the water on impact had flipped the built-in white bra outside of my swimsuit. My Esther Williams's dive had flipped my two falsies from my bathing suit bra top to the water's surface. I had no choice but to dive under the water and return my built-in bra back to its original position inside the Jantzen, while the New River gang fought hard not to snicker.

My face matched my swimsuit color and Junior's scarlet belly and back-buster body. Rachel Ann was not even trying to conceal her amusement. And to make matters worse, Dubs was winking at me again. I couldn't even enjoy it. I vowed to listen to my mama more from that day forward. I had to start acting like a lady. This showing out had gotten me a wink, but my pride had been squashed in front of the first boy I ever loved.

The return trip to Aunt May's was the longest trip ever. I was too embarrassed to make eye contact with any of the Valiant's passengers. I replayed Mama's advice in my head over and over again, "*Ducky Pearman, you are a woman now, so conduct yourself like one. Humility follows vanity.*" Sure did. She was right on both counts.

The summer went too quickly. I knew winter in Tennessee would not be as hard on me, but the words of Albert Camus from my English lit book would comfort me, "In the depths of winter, I discovered within me, an invincible summer." The harsh mountain weather would never hamper my thoughts of the splendid summers I spent on the New River. I just knew the author of this quote must have experienced splendid summers, too. To speak these wise words could only mean one thing in my mind—love. Albert Camus had a summer love, just like I had with Dubs. I had memories of my first invincible summer to temper any chill—all in one wink of a teenaged boy's thick-lashed eye.

I made my I-81 trip with Uncle Emmett back to the River Valley in Tennessee. Rose had married her high school sweetheart in a small church wedding while I had been away that summer. I was sad that I missed Rose's wedding. Since mama didn't drive and Uncle Emmett was busy selling cars, the trip back to Tennessee was not to be. I don't think Rose would have married so early, but she was a very responsible sister, according to my mother, and wanted a home of her own with more privacy and respect than she got from us. I wasn't there, but sisters Kate and Helen were full of details of Rose's church wedding and fellowship hall reception. Our small mountain community made a great turn out—church was a social gathering. Mama made it special for her and invited all 192 church members. Most came. Rose finally got something just for her—a wedding, a reception, and her lifetime love James.

Privacy didn't happen with a house full of noisy kids. We prowled in all of Rose's things. Heck, some of the best times Kate, Helen, and I had were going through Rose's cedar hope chest. We tried on all her clothes, especially her high-heeled shoes, her Avon pearl pendant, and her robe for the wedding night. We read personal notes, looked into boxes, and marked a mustache on every boy in her class of 1955 Cyclone yearbook. We were rude and disrespectful. No wonder Rose wanted to get away from us.

Her hope was not in the chest but in the fact that she hooked James before we completely wore out all her items placed there. She hoped, all right. She hoped to get away from the likes of three noisy, aggravating younger sisters.

Rose never had exactly a "normal" childhood. She had to grow up much too soon. After Daddy had died in the living room, Rose stepped in to help Mama with us three. We were under the age of six when Daddy went away. I preferred to give that answer when asked about his whereabouts- that he was away on a trip, not dead. I left the part out about it being a permanent trip, and that he ain't coming back any time soon. I thought it sounded rather good to put a spin on his death; it didn't sound final or as hurtful as the word "death" to a five-year-old. Rose was part mother, seamstress, chauffeur, and friend to us before her sixteenth birthday. She remained like a mother hen to us for the rest of her life. Sisters are gifts to be cherished. They share a bloodline that bonds infinitely.

Howard, our only brother, was a football player, a fisherman, and a favorite of most who knew him. He was Rose's favorite sibling. He was good, too. He also had one of those magnetic personalities. My mama and aunts adored him. He had a mannerism that separated him from the rest of us. If he liked you and came to talk to you, he would get close to your right side and take your earlobe between his thumb and index finger and rub it while talking. He did this as a child instead of using a pacifier or having a "blanky." The earlobe rubbing was an integral part of his mannerisms. He did it as one would breathe—an involuntary action. He never let the fact he was a teenager deter him. Howard was the only student I ever knew who had friends from the country and friends from the city high schools at the same time. His personality attracted most everyone

I can remember vividly the week after Howard graduated from high school. He came into my mama's high-ceilinged blue bedroom. When family talks occurred, they were always held in Mama's blue bedroom. Howard asked us all to be in attendance in Mama's meeting room.

He stood there, all 145 pounds of him, with dark brown eyes like Mama's, Kate's, Helen's, and mine.

"Mama, you know I love you and the girls, don't you?"

I had already figured out the news would not be good. Mama's face twisted and she rested on her stomach, one over the other.

Howard continued, "Rose is married now, and I feel I need to move on with my life, too."

Mama interrupted him, "Howard, you know you don't need to do anything differently but go on to school and stay right here with me and your sisters."

We were eligible for the GI Bill. Rose attended the same college mama had graduated from. Rose was going to school on the GI Bill, even though she was married. Why not Howard? Why could he not have been in step with the pattern already begun by Rose and Mama? However, the pattern was not to be.

"I know," said Howard. "But I have already made a decision. I have joined the Air Force."

Mama raised her hands and grabbed hold of the oak mantel above the fireplace. She leaned her head on her right arm and uttered in the saddest voice, "Son, if you do that, we will never see you again." Her words were a premonition when voiced to us that day. We girls did not know it at the time, but Mama did.

I will never forget Howard with us in the bedroom at the fireplace. My sisters and I didn't say a word. We just grabbed him around the legs and tried to hold him to us as long as he stood there.

As I looked out of the corner of my eye, I saw tears falling from Rose and Mama's faces. Mama was losing a son and Rose, her best friend and confidante.

We all shed tears the day he left with his duffel bag, walking to catch the Greyhound bus. Howard never looked back after the last hug and kiss he gave each of us. That would be the last time we saw him except for Rose. She made James drive her all the way to South Dakota when he graduated from flight school. She was the lucky one, the one who got to hug him again right before he went away—just like my Daddy had. Never to return.

When school started that year, I was a freshman at age twelve, but in November, I would become a teenager. Never would I have realized what kind of a beginning high school would be for me. It didn't have to do with making good grades, either.

Good grades had been easy for my sisters and me. We took academic qualifying tests to get the GI Bill, and we did so as each graduated high school successfully. It was a good thing, too, because Mama would later have three girls in college at the same time.

One of the teachers announced: "If your name begins with the letters 'O' through 'T,' then go with Mrs. Edens to your assigned homeroom."

I had heard about Mrs. Edens. She was the teacher I had hoped for to start each day. Also, I was in the same homeroom with my best friends, Constance Street and Lexie Phillips. The schedule and the alphabet were working in my favor. It was going to be a good year.

An abrupt interruption came. The school office receptionist's voice boomed, "Jessica Pearman, please come to the office."

My heart almost stopped. Was I in some kind of trouble on the first day of school? I nervously left the old gym, and as I made my way to the hallway, I could see a small group of people huddled together by the principal's office. As I moved closer, I saw my brother-in-law James and Howard's best friend, Dale.

I felt it to my bones that something was wrong. It had to be Mama. I started praying as I walked. The group separated as I approached. They had been crying, too.

The others turned and shook their head as if to be saying, "You poor girl. You poor, poor girl."

My brother-in-law took one hand; my brother's friend took the other hand. I saw Kate moving toward us, and she looked as forlorn as I felt. Not a word was said until we slid inside the white 1962 Chevy Impala.

We climbed into the backseat. Kate looked at me, gaunt and sad, with her dark eyes set in a pool of tears. She grabbed my hand, and for Kate this was huge, because she was an ill sort of person and did not reveal much emotion unless to scream at Helen or me. For the first time, I saw Kate was as scared as I.

Together, not even knowing what the other one was thinking, we asked, "James, is it Mama?"

James and Dale did not answer. They shook their heads sideways. They could not find the words to tell us. We drove along in total silence except for Kate's and my sniffling. We were looking dread in the eyes without knowing the root of it.

As we topped the hill to descend to the old white clapboard house with the tin roof, we saw Rose first, then Helen, who had been at the nearby elementary school, then two of our aunts and a half dozen neighbors on the wraparound gray porch. More people. All dressed in a veil of sadness.

Dale helped to get us from the Impala. Our ears met the most heartrending sobs from our mama. As Kate and I ran to her, she had a crumpled telegram in her hand from the United States government. I read it with Kate.

Howard would never be returning to the River Doe, to us, or to Mama. He was killed in an airplane crash with fifty-four other military enlistees. The aircraft he was aboard had crashed into a mountain as it was coming into Spokane, Washington. My heart sank. My daddy, now my brother? Why? I knew nothing would be quite the same after this family-shattering news. And it never was. Howard was dearly loved. Most of our table conversations with mama were updates about Howard that we relished while eating supper. It had become our ritual since he had joined the Air Force. What could we possibly talk about now?

I looked for Kate and saw her running toward the woods above our mountain valley house. She was headed in the direction of her "quiet and alone place." Helen and I were forbidden to trespass on Kate's secret spot. Since she was next in age to Howard, I knew she would grieve, and most would never know the depth of her anguish. Kate was like that. She internalized her emotions.

On the other hand, poor Helen and I were crying inconsolably. We were afraid. Our mama had never shown us sadness. Her face was one of consistency and strength. Now, it was contorted, and she sobbed deep and long sitting in our old rickety front porch swing. Rose tried to hold mama in her arms. Rose's face was ashen. Howard was five years younger than Rose. She considered him her closest sibling. No matter how tightly Rose held mama around the shoulders, mama just sat with her face looking downward and calling Howard's name. "Howard, oh, Howard, my fine son." Her shoulders stooped never to rise as upright again. She appeared to age right in front of us. This hurt seemed even deeper than the loss of my daddy for each of us.

We buried our only brother beside our daddy. The bugler played "Taps." The 21-rifle shots thundered in our ears and offered finality to the horrific loss to our lives.

Our mama was left with three girls in a home devoid of men. She never married again and never expressed any interest in men after that. The two she had loved with all her heart had abandoned her without a word. The sting of it all never left her, cloaking her life with the deepest of hurt.

We never saw Mama cry for Howard again after he was laid to rest at Union Cemetery in my daddy's family plot in Jonesborough. But we heard her cry every night from the privacy of the blue bedroom.

I questioned, "Mama, what is it like to lose a child?"

She put her arms around me and pulled me close to her heart, to a place where I could hear it beat. She looked toward the bedroom where my brother had slept for the nineteen years of his too-brief life, and said, "Part of your heart dies along with that child, Ducky." He was a sweet brother, and his death caused a huge void in our lives and an irreplaceable hole in my mama's heart.

I believed her.

I loved my mama. I felt her pain over and over. I felt a little guilty about Howard's death, because I subconsciously had been relieved it had not been Mama. That night I cried myself to sleep, not because my mama had lost part of her heart, but because nothing I could ever do in this old world would ever put it back together. She silently grieved for my brother, her only son, until her death at eighty-one. A small drawer containing his picture, a Bulldog yearbook, and a pillowcase he sent her from the training base were in an old mahogany desk in the living room. When the drawer was slightly pulled away from its closure, I knew my mama had been in thought with Howard. The drawer was always ajar in the early morning when we came down the stairs to eat breakfast. No words were spoken about the contents of the drawer until after her death. We respected her time to grieve for our brother in the stillness of the morning. My sisters and I never invaded the desk drawer, either. That was respectfully reserved for Mama.

Summer finally arrived. The past year had taken a toll on our family. I thought about staying on the River Doe this summer, but Mama encouraged me to go to Aunt May's. She had made it appear that Aunt May and Uncle Art couldn't do without me. It didn't take much convincing. I was thirteen now and anxious to see my New River friends and Virginia family. When Uncle Emmett pulled into Aunt May's and Uncle Art's driveway, I noticed a gigantic white-streaked and weathered canvas tent blocking my view of the Jennings's house. Was it a circus? I needed to investigate the monstrosity that had appeared this summer.

Aunt May was quick to tell me the Holiness was having a tent revival. I had never seen one, and I figured if the Jennings and the Stoots attended, I would, too. We could have watched all the goings on in the tent from Uncle Art's porch if the tent's front flap had been left up. It never was. I supposed they wanted people to come inside the tent, not sit outside on a plank porch under the crab apple trees and gawk.

The Holiness wanted everyone to come to the revival. They counted on converting others of different religions or no religion to the Holiness flock. I figured a tent was a good start to getting everyone's attention. Aunt May and Uncle Art were Methodists. Mama was one, too. I had been baptized in the Valley Forge Christian Church nearest our house since my mama didn't drive, and we could walk to it.

Next to diving, I was next best at church. If Dubs thought my diving was good, he was going to be more impressed with my spirituality. I was born with an active spiritual consciousness. I always felt better when I had gone to church. Aunt May loved my spiritual side. I loved hers. She took me to Vacation Bible School. As I got older, she depended on me as her helper. One way or another, I had to be in church. She was always working on a project for the Methodists and praying.

I went to tell her good night once and found her on her knees at the end of the bed praying. Uncle Art was snoring loudly, but Aunt May continued her vigil anyway. She prayed every night at the end of the bed.

She told me when she grew up that it was common for God-fearing people to have a family praying altar. She said her daddy, who she referred to as "Poppa," and mother, my grandparents, had an altar in their home and had a family altar prayer every single night.

From that day forward when I was in Aunt May's house, I knelt and prayed before climbing into bed. I felt it was out of respect to God as well as Aunt May. This was a habit I cultivated and kept repeating while visiting in Austinville.

The only reason I didn't continue the kneeling practice in the Tennessee Mountains was I was afraid I would freeze to the ice cold floors in our house in the winter like my tongue had stuck to an orange Popsicle once. When bedtime arrived in the mountains, neither my sisters nor I tarried on a cold floor. I had to relegate my altar praying to table praying at mealtime. I prayed the Lord would take the Popsicle situation into consideration and forgive me my transgression for the sin of altar praying omission.

"Ducky, you want to go over to the tent revival?" asked Sue Ann Stoots.

"I do, Sue Ann, if Aunt May lets me." I figured my chances were pretty good with her religious history. Since the tent was in the lower part of the Jennings's field, I was pretty sure Dubs would be in attendance or at least nearby. I had a winning situation; either way, it got me closer to his house.

I found the whole experience interesting. I couldn't find many similarities between Methodists church goers and Holiness ones. These Holinesses meant business. They answered when Brother Houston asked a question. Methodist church members didn't. Holinesses waved hands, stood up during the preaching, and spoke inaudible languages called tongues. Methodist people didn't.

This proved interesting as I quit listening to Brother Houston and just watched all the Holiness action.

If a sister yelled out, and I didn't see it coming, I would almost jump out of my skin like all the other kids. Also, the more the Holiness members talked or spoke in tongues during the service, the more the evangelist talked and the longer the tent revival night. The tent revival was no quick service. People stayed until they looked too tired to ask another question, wave another hand, or yell another, "Amen, brother, tell it like it is."

Just as I was losing interest in the Holiness, Brother Houston announced a new Holy Bible would be given to the young person eighteen or younger that could say from memory the most verses from the Holy Bible.

He used a hook to get us interested. Then he said, "Every night, starting Tuesday until Friday, we will close the service with Bible verses by our young people."

I listened intently. It was a Bible verse competition, and I loved competitions. Sue Ann and I did a high five and went to our respective homes to start memorizing.

I couldn't wait to tell Aunt May, who had been with Mrs. Jennings sitting on the porch and listening to the whole service. I think the people in Wytheville and Cripple Creek, twenty miles away, heard it, too.

I wanted to make Aunt May proud. I didn't need a new Holy Bible, because my King James Version was still in good condition, but it was a competition after all. I heard Aunt May tell Uncle Art when he came to bed, "That little dickens might win that Bible, Art!"

I must have been "that little dickens" she was talking about, which made me proud.

Uncle Art had stayed in the barbershop, cleaning up as long as he could. He wanted none of the Holiness's "shenanigans." I heard him snoring just as her praying commenced.

"Jesus wept. The meek shall inherit the earth." I continued onward, using a strategy to get the easy ones out of the way and raise my number of verses said.

Then I threw in Proverbs 31:13: "She seekest wool, and flax, and workest willingly with her hands." This one was a tribute to Aunt May and her Singer sewing machine. I decided to do twenty verses a night. And I did.

I inventoried my competition. Sue Ann Stoots appeared to be the toughest contender.

Junior and Dubs told me they went to church on Sunday, and that was enough church for one week. It was a good thing, too, because if Dubs had come, I probably would have lacked Bible verse focus. Dubs had a way of fogging my brain that even God could not defrost.

Jr. and Dubs had Virginia driver learner's permits now and spent all their time trying to get a turn at their daddy's cars when Mr. Jennings and Mr. Lefpher came home from working shifts at the Norfork and Pacific Railroad depot in Bristol.

By the third night of the tent revival, I had eliminated all the Holiness kids and was in progress to out-memorize Sue Ann Stoots. She knew it. I knew it, and the Holiness knew it. By the close of Thursday's night service, I was comfortably in the lead.

I recounted each night's successes with Aunt May and Mrs. Jennings on the porch after the revival. These two proved my most supportive fans. Aunt May would do an instant replay, "Ducky's a shoe-in, Art," then she would start praying, and he would start snoring.

I was almost asleep as I heard the rain slap against my screened window. The tent revival had zapped my energy.

Jessie Shields Strickland

I faintly heard Junior and Dubs laugh as they passed Aunt May's house. I learned the following day that they had sneaked from their house to collect night crawlers for fishing.

I slept well that night and dreamt of accepting my shiny black leather Holy Bible from the Holiness, followed by the melodic, distinct, and distant laugh of Dubs Jennings. I slept like a baby.

Friday night, the last revival night, came to the Holiness tent. Aunt May had made me a new skirt; it was a light pink, whip stitched one to wear with a white Dr. Kildare-type shirt with a high neckline that buttoned down the right side. My long brown hair had been washed, dried, curled, and brushed until it shined. I would have put on my watermelon-flavored lip gloss, but the Holiness were not much for makeup. I did without and kept it simple.

Inside the revival tent, Brother Houston was about to do the altar call when I noticed Pam Stoots to the left of the tent. I had not seen her in the tent before tonight. As soon as he finished, which was not quick enough for me, he asked anyone who had Bible verses to say to come say them for the last time and then a winner would be announced.

He didn't seem too happy about a Tennessee, part-Methodist, part-Christian member about to win the Bible.

I had my twenty verses ready from Psalm's Chapter 78. I was planning to make it a grand finale. I got through quickly, and no one else seemed to be coming forward. After all, hadn't I eliminated the Holinesses, Baptists, Methodists, and Presbyterians that had come to the New River revival?

I was letting my vanity seep again. Just when Brother Houston started to present me the new Bible, he stopped. I looked up, and coming to the front was a sturdily built, older girl, rather thick eye-browed and sporting a gap-toothed smile. It was none other than the very Dodger herself, Pam Stoots.

I could not see how Pam Stoots could possibly beat my record of sixty verses. She had to say at least sixty-one to take the new Bible. Was this fair? It must have been. No Holiness stopped her. They sat there with smug expressions plastered on their Holiness faces.

Pam Stoots stood as composed as one who could smell victory. She began within Matthew, and by the time she reached Chapter 11:15, she looked right at me on the sixty-second verse and finished in her deep voice, "He who has ears to hear, let him hear." She took the once-coveted Holy Bible from Brother Houston as the Holiness applauded her while she sauntered through the tent flap exit.

The tent revival was concluded. Pam Stoots had walked away with the new Holy Bible meant for me. She had been the secret weapon of the Holiness—a Dodger and Holiness! I moved humbly from the tent. I had to put my hands over my ears to halt the ringing of Mama's words, "Ducky, humility follows vanity."

I mumbled, "Oh, Lord, it is hard to be humble after being publicly humiliated by a Holiness Dodger!"

I finally grasped her wise words. For the second time in two years, vanity had whipped me. I uttered dejectedly and quietly, "I got it now, Mama. I got it!"

I walked across the paved road, traveling no more than fifty yards from the tent to the front porch. I was devastated. Aunt May and Mrs. Jennings had already heard from the Holiness leaving the tent after the winner Pam Stoot's departure and her "laying it on the Tennessee Methodist Christian church kid." Mrs. Jennings made a few feeble attempts to make me feel better. Then she left. Aunt May was at a loss for words since she had believed I was a "shoe-in."

Uncle Art had pretended not to have kept up with the tent's nightly events. He saved the day. Holding his large hand out to pat the top of my head ever so compassionately, he forged on with, "Ducky, girl, I never did like those Holiness anyway. You just can't trust a one of them."

Uncle Art was a man of few words. Right there on the porch, I knew exactly why God said, "The meek shall inherit the earth." It was God's way to reward people on the earth just like my Uncle Art who were humble. Amen.

Filled with another dose of good, Dubs, and some not-so-good, the tent revival thrashing, memories from the New River, I returned with Uncle Emmett to Tennessee. I had wanted Mama and the girls to experience good memories from their summer, too.

They had. I knew Mama would never get over Howard's death, but maybe she could make peace with the US government as time passed. She held them partly responsible.

Mama had spent many days with Kate and Helen at a mountain spring-fed swimming pool in the nearby community of Brammer. Mama knew the lady proprietor, Mrs. Heaton. My sisters helped her two beautiful daughters in the dressing room locker areas. They would oversee the lockers, straighten the bathroom areas when unoccupied, or lifeguard the kiddie pool—whatever needed to be done. To be seen with the Heaton girls was good for high schoolers in training. Kate and Helen had fun summers, too.

James would drive them to the swimming pool each day except Sunday, church day, and Monday, wash day.

Mama helped Mrs. Heaton in concessions to pay for season tickets for Kate and Helen. At the end of the day, James or Rose would come back the six miles and get them. Mrs. Heaton and her two daughters knew Howard and thought this would help Mama to pass the time rather than staying home thinking about him. Neighbors do that for neighbors in smaller communities. No one has to grieve alone.

"Ducky, you should have seen it," Helen said excitedly. "Mrs. Heaton had to go to the end of the pool deck and scream, 'Mr. Simpkins, you can't be on the rock taking a bath! You need to get out now!'"

In the shallow end of the Olympic-sized Brammer swimming pool was a huge sky-blue boulder used as a resting place for the tired novice swimmers, a meeting place for teenaged girls, or a horseplay "King of the Rock" retreat for pre-adolescent boys. It was never meant to be a rock for bathing as Helen described.

She recounted the story down to Mr. Simpkin's paying admission, jumping in the cold water, dog-paddling to the rock, and digging the bar of Lava soap hidden in one of his cut-off and ragged-edged blue jean short's pockets.

He preceded to suds his body on the rock in plain view of all the paying swimmers, about two dozen. Mrs. Heaton had confiscated Mr. Simpkin's bar of Lava soap on his hasty exit from the pool. Mrs. Heaton was a no-nonsense business lady and wasn't about to let a soiled farmer clean up in the pool, even if she had to refund his fifty cents.

Mama, Kate, and Helen had lovely tales to share about the pool goers. I listened to them all, even the one with Kate getting to ride over Brammer in Buddy Carter's family airplane. Kate excitedly had tossed her red gingham bathing suit cover-up from the window, hoping to signal to the pool goers below of her adventure. Needless to say, no one in the three county areas ever reported finding Kate's cover-up. Kate was humbled by the experience.

"Ducky, did you have a good summer with Uncle Art and Aunt May?"

I usually didn't tell them much, but I wanted to this year. I told them about Hungry Mother State Park, especially the part about my diving. I omitted the part about my bathing suit mishap and Dubs Jennings holding my hand. I gave them the whole scoop about Pam Stoots knocking me out of the Holy Bible verse championship. We had many good laughs. The sharing of our summer tales of 1962 sustained us through the cold and harsh Tennessee mountain winter.

Early spring, Mama made a decision to buy Kate a car. It was the first family car we had owned since my daddy's death. Mama did not like to depend on James or Rose for all our transportation, even though I never heard either complain.

James taught Kate to drive a banana yellow-colored Chevrolet Corvair, with a stick shift, around the curviest roads in Carter County above Little Wilbur dam road to the Lookout.

He said, "Kate, if you can drive to the lookout, you can pass the driver's test at the state patrol office."

The road to the lookout, a scenic Tennessee Valley Authority Park clearing with a panoramic vista of the Watauga Lake, was as curvy and twisting as a coiled black snake that lurked along the banks of the winding Doe River.

James added, "The road test will be no problem, but learning the *Tennessee Highway Patrol Driver's Manual* is up to you. You are on your own with it, so study the road rules."

James could have kept his words to himself on this advice, because Kate was determined to pass the driver's test—road and manual. Mama said if Kate had applied her studying to biology like she had to the driver's test, she would have passed it. Kate knew biology subject matter, but it was the yearly dissection of the asexual earthworm and her fainting that caused her biology grade to plummet. No earthworms to dissect made the driver's test a cinch. Kate passed her driver's test with flying colors. Now, she needed a car to put her driving skills to use.

Mama had been known as a wise woman until she let Kate select the family car. Mama admitted later she let Kate do the picking, because she only knew about Packards.

None of us had ever heard of a Packard, so we thought she did need help in choosing a car—just not from Kate.

Kate ordered a new navy sloped-back car called a Barracuda made by Plymouth. It came with a stick shift, which Kate knew some about, and a Hemi engine. Kate was clueless on the power she was about to encounter.

A young, slick-talking salesman wearing a light blue leisure suit convinced Kate and Mama a Hemi-equipped Barracuda fastback was the way to go.

A beginner driver should never be given access to a Hemi, two-door bucket seat car with a five-speed gear system and an eight-cylinder, jet-fueled engine that could reach speeds up to 180 mph. The two large white racing stripes going from bumper across to bumper on the Barracuda called, "Come drag race with me!"

Kate rose from dateless status to mountain boys standing in line. Every boy from Elizabethton to Brammar wanted a chance at the wheel of a Formula S Barracuda and all that horsepower. Kate became "the girl" to be seen with. She was a dude and chick magnet—girls loved the attention the boys gave them when riding inside the Barracuda; boys loved the feeling of power behind the wheel of it as they fantasized about being a Fireball Roberts NASCAR racer for an evening. Kate's Barracuda was loved by them all—except the "county mounty" or "po-po," better known as the police.

Mama, Helen, and I just wanted peace restored and one trip to Gurney's Burger Place. All Mama got was three new clutches, many police warnings, and two speeding tickets to pay for Kate, and a lousy price on a trade-in.

Kate practically destroyed the car in three months. Other mamas forbade their children from riding with her. Much of her popularity had gone out the window along with the trade-in.

Mama made a much wiser decision about cars after that. She ordered from an older salesman in a dark suit and went with a four-door, 120 mph max, shell blue-colored automatic Chevy II, and it cut Kate's popularity in half.

We got Gurney burgers every Friday as a family, and Mama actually got to see a return for her money. Kate was a "handful" after that, Mama said. Truly. She had tasted the wild side. And she had liked it.

Another hot, lazy summer drifted in along with the fragrant honeysuckle wind.

On my ride to Virginia, I got Uncle Emmett to open up to me about his life. I picked up the nerve to pry as to why he had married so many women. He had five marriages, one didn't count after it was recalled or annulled.

Mama wasn't around to shush me up, either.

He seemed to deliberate over his answer, then shared that he kept thinking he would find the right one, so he kept on looking. But he never did.

The one he loved and had married didn't love him back. She had given birth to his only two children, who were grown now and married.

This was more like it. He was releasing some good information. I was sure he was telling me his deep dark secrets, and I would have crossed my heart and hoped to have choked if I would breathe a one of his secrets. I was mesmerized by his candidness and just knew he would feel better to get out all the deep secrets. I continued with some empathy and much zeal.

I queried, "Uncle Emmett, will you love her until you die?"

He said solemnly, "Yes, Ducky. I will."

I forged on with my inquisition. "Did you ever see her again after you divorced her?"

"No, Ducky. I have not." Now, that was the saddest thing I had ever heard.

I asked, "What was she like?"

"Belle was a beautiful woman, spoiled by a family who had revolved around her every need or want. She wasn't much of a wife."

"Was she a good mother, then?" *Surely she had one redeeming quality,* I thought.

"She was a worse mother than wife, and for that, I could not stay married to her, Ducky." He went on, "But then, I haven't been much of a father, either. Caroline and Inez had to practically raise themselves. Her family favored Inez, who looked just like Belle. Inez's life was good. Poor Caroline stayed with Papa Pack on the farm while I kept working in Roanoke to support her in a way she was accustomed and expected. Papa Pack didn't have a bed for Caroline. He made her one from a coffin bottom. Caroline never complained."

"Caroline was the nicest girl," Uncle Emmett said as he seemed somewhere else other than on I-81. "She never was a minute's trouble. Life was not fair to her back then. She has a better life now, Ducky—married a boat captain near Chesapeake Bay. She is surrounded by a family that loves her."

I thought to myself, *I am sure glad of that.* Imagine sleeping in a coffin before your time comes. I got goose bumps from even thinking about it. I decided my prying hadn't gotten me anywhere. Uncle Emmett was lost in his thoughts about unrequited love and lost fatherhood. I was depressed to think of my lovely, kind cousin Caroline sleeping in a dadgum coffin before her time.

Nosiness must be akin to vanity. I was humbled to have not one but two good homes and beds for sleep. I was more than glad to reach New River.

As I got my annual squeeze from Aunt May and my pat on the head from Uncle Art, I was anxious to find out what had been happening to my New River friends.

The first friend I saw was not Dubs, as I had hoped to see, but my best female friend, fellow Yankee baseball player Sue Ann Stoots. She came on the porch to talk to me and to ask if I would walk with her to Jenelle's store to get items her mama needed in the kitchen. I eagerly looked for my permission nod from Aunt May. I got my nod. I kissed Uncle Emmett, Aunt May, and Uncle Art on their cheeks. Uncle Emmett winked at me. I guess that meant Unk wasn't mad for all the meddling I had done in his personal business on this trip. I felt relieved. All that personal stuff made us have a stronger connection. He had let me glimpse at a past no one got to see or hear about. Uncle Emmett was like Aunt May and my mama, which was a family tradition to keep your mouth shut and let the past be, just that, the past.

Somehow my I-81 conversation made me feel closer to Uncle Emmett. None had been brave enough to question his life. I knew he would be gone when I returned. He had to drive the additional hour to his house in Roanoke. I was comforted to know Aunt May would send him on his journey with one of her lovely, nourishing meals. Food was a Southern soul-soother, especially at Aunt May's home.

Off Sue Ann and I went, giggling at the thought of another summer together.

Sue Ann couldn't wait to tell me Dubs Jennings was going to asked me to his prom at Fort Chatwell High School at the end of the approaching school year. Dubs was a senior and would be graduating. I was a junior. The very thought of the prom invitation made me giddy with sheer delight.

I found, even though Dubs and Junior had bona fide driver's licenses that summer, they still liked to fish, play baseball, and pull pranks. Boys were pretty much boys, even with drivers licenses, I discovered from those two.

One night, I discovered firsthand their boyish ways. Sue Ann, Dubs, and Junior were outside my screened window whispering, "Ducky, are you awake?"

"Yes, shh, or you'll wake Uncle Art and Aunt May."

Sue Ann whispered, "Come outside."

"Are you crazy?" I muttered.

"No, we need you to help us for about fifteen minutes."

I should have known nothing good could come from four teenagers sneaking out of their houses at night, but decision time was upon me, and making a teenage judgment call, I whispered, "I will, but only for fifteen minutes."

Since only a few people ever locked their doors in the South at night in the early '60s, I figured I could walk through the living room quietly through the unlocked door and come back again without waking my aunt and uncle. Uncle Art's snoring, whistles, and snorts would aid my cause, since his sounds could muffle a dog barking. Tonight was one of his louder nights, and I prayed that my friends did not hear him. Aunt May was use to it after thirty-five years of marriage. I, on the other hand, was not but would never complain about it again. When you needed Uncle Art the most, he seemed to always come through, even when he wasn't aware of it.

I slipped on my khaki shorts and then slid over my head the nautical shirt Aunt May had made me. I tied the shoelaces on my Keds and moved quietly toward the living room.

I tiptoed to the door, turned the knob ever so gently, and exited from the safety of the house into the eerie summer night's darkness, guided by the soft moonlight and my friend Sue Ann's urging onward, with her hand pushing on my arm.

Dubs had a flashlight. He did not turn it on, as the moon was full. Sue Ann hung onto my arm until my eyes adjusted to the surroundings of the night.

"Where are we going? Why are we going out at night? Aren't you afraid we'll get caught?"

"Ducky, don't asked so many questions," Dubs said. "We'll tell you when we get there."

By the familiar bushes and trail by the barbershop, it looked like we were headed for New River Bridge. As we arrived at the bridge, Dubs told Sue Ann, Junior, and me to stay on the left side of the road near the hydrangeas at the border of the Jennings's yard.

Dubs and Jr. had work to do. Sue Ann and I were told to be sentries for a porch light to come on or a vehicle to come by. We could do that job.

We hid behind the hydrangeas as we served as lookouts and watched Dubs and Jr. pull up a plank from the pedestrian side of the bridge floor. It was a plank from the beginning of the walkway, not over the water. The plank was tossed to the side.

I had an instant twinge of remorse, wishing I had stayed in the comfort of my aunt's soft down bedding; however, it was a fleeting pang. I still didn't see a problem, as I could return the plank the boys had thrown to the side when I made my daily sojourn in the morning to the store for Aunt May.

We left the "crime" scene. True to Dub's word, we were back within fifteen minutes. I didn't ask any more questions since I was anxious to return to my bed without being missed. I knew I would not be able to come back to my summer home without my mama if my relatives knew I had slipped out of their house. A pulled-up plank certainly didn't seem like it was worth giving up my idyllic summers, aunt and uncle's kindness, fabulous meals, and Dubs.

I couldn't sleep for worrying about the plank and the possibility of Aunt May and Uncle Art never trusting me again. That spiritual conscience finally kicked into gear about fifteen minutes too late, but I was relieved it did make an appearance, with a healthy dose of guilt as its sidekick.

I finally drifted off in the wee hours of the morning, only to be awakened by the smell of stewed cinnamon apples and the sound of crackling country ham in the skillet. This woman could cook.

I watched sewing customers come and go all morning. Lying on Aunt May's daybed in her sewing room, and relaxed by the idle throttle of her Singer, I read part of a paperback by Agatha Christie I had found on Aunt May's bookshelf. I was in mystery mode, as I still had not solved the missing plank crime, even if I was an accessory. My activated Methodist conscience was prodding restless and anxious thoughts.

What if the missing plank caused an accident? What if I could not get to the bridge in time to replace the plank? Why wasn't Aunt May sending me to Janelle's like she did each morning? Worst of all, what if Tuny Fisher's mama, when she came to collect her sewing repairs, had seen us from her bedroom window that faced the bridge and told Aunt May? I felt unkind emotions flood over me like the River Doe does the rocks after a nasty spring rain. All morning I tossed like a salad. I never got to leave the house. This was a prime day of the month, payday for most of the new River families, and Aunt May was bombarded by the ladies who were retrieving their sewing repair items. Aunt May gave her full concentration to each, and collected a meager amount from each. She was a bargain and a jewel in the community, my Aunt May.

When lunch came, Uncle Art sat at the head of the table, which was customary, and he was more talkative than usual, which was not customary. He relayed a story one of his customer's had told before lunch break. The customer, Mr. Lefphew, was taking a leave day from the railroad depot in Bristol and needed a haircut.

"May, Mr. Lefphew told me in the shop this morning as Joe Mills was coming home last night from the late shift in the limestone mine, he went through a hole in the bridge."

Oh, my goodness, ye sins shall find ye out, or something like that—this was Peter, Jr.'s father! If he only knew—his namesake was part of the crime scene. Lordy, no wonder my emotions were off. My Methodist conscience was trying to warn me about the events to come. I was just too wrapped up in my thoughts of Dubs to see it. One indiscretion and boom! Life, as I knew it, might be changed forever.

I couldn't believe my ears. Joe "Boney" Mills was about six feet and didn't look to weigh 100 pounds soaking wet. His ears were the largest visible part of his body.

"May, if it hadn't been for his metal dinner box getting crossways between the planks which stopped his fall, he could have gotten seriously hurt."

"How hurt was he, Uncle Art?" I whimpered.

"A few scratches and bruises, Ducky, but mostly it just scared him. He got those when he turned loose of the dinner box leather strap handle and fell into the bushes on the river bank." *Relief, relief,* I thought. At least he wasn't killed or seriously injured by our childish foolishness. Bruised was bad enough.

I could not eat another bite. Aunt May was trying to figure out how the plank was missing, and no one had noticed. Uncle Art was intrigued with Joe "Boney's" body being thin enough to go all the way through the narrow hole. I was scared by the thought of being caught as one who helped in the plank scheme.

I was an eyewitness to it all. I could solve Aunt May's query along with Uncle Art's. But dare I? Not in this lifetime.

I had once been known as the peacemaker, the "no trouble" girl. I was ashamed of myself for the first time in my life. I knew how Hester Prynne in the *Scarlet Letter*, wearing the "A" for "Adultery" in harsh public punishment, must have felt.

Shame was truly worse than vanity or nosiness. I saw myself in an unflattering orange one-piece jumpsuit with "Prisoner" emblazoned on the back of it.

What would happen to me? My friends? I had no one to blame for this but myself. I knew better. I was a disgrace to my mama's good Methodist raising.

My dear God, what had I done? Aunt May would be devastated to have her favorite niece fallen from grace. I could forget about Uncle Art's head pats, too. He was meek and kind, but he would not abide the likes of me, an accessory to the missing plank crime, if he discovered my whereabouts on "crime night." The Holiness would never let my family live this down.

Aunt May might as well have stitched me a big red "PS" for "Plank Sinner" on my lovely nautical white-and-navy-striped shirt she had so generously made me on the Singer. I would never be able to wear that shirt without remembering my being a willing participant

Jessie Shields Strickland

to almost seriously hurting this unassuming man who wouldn't hurt a flea.

At that moment, I knew I was not cut out for crime.

I found out my friends weren't, either. Dubs and Jr. thought it was sorta funny when they first heard it from their parents, until they replayed the situation and realized Joe "Boney" could have been seriously hurt. They regretted it some, I could tell. I knew they would certainly regret getting caught.

Sue Ann was in as terrible a state as I. After all, her sister was the Holiness Holy Bible verse champ, Pam Stoots. If Pam ever found out Sue Ann was involved in the Joe Mill's "unfortunate accident," known to four teenagers as the "plank crime," she would have made us all pay. Pam could have whipped all four of us with one arm tied behind her.

The talk of New River was Joe "Boney" Mills going through the New River Bridge's missing plank hole.

The more the New River neighbors passed the story along, the more embellished it became. Listening to the magnitude of Joe Mills' story revision made it keep going. The community spread this like they did their apple butter on white bread, the thicker the better.

Joe was supposedly left hanging from his dinner box the rest of the night. He was said to have dropped in the river, and the current washed him to the New River Shot Tower, where ammunition for the settlers had been made about 130 years ago. They said he walked twelve miles from the tower to get back home.

Joe "Boney" became an overnight hero. The saga of the missing plank spread, as did Joe's popularity and heroism.

No one ever queried how the plank got removed but Aunt May. She gave her questioning up as people became more interested in seeing a man thin enough who could fit through a plank hole, dangle for hours in midair, and survive. They wanted to see the metal dinner box, too, with the black leather handle still hanging and attached.

The New River Bridge had never gotten so much publicity or visitors. Joe "Boney" had never experienced so much attention either. My friends and I started to ease up on our guilt with Joe "Boney's" fame. The orange jumpsuit image faded. God did have mercy on sinners, especially four novice teenage pranksters.

Dubs Jenning's dad and mom asked Aunt May and Uncle Art if I could go to Wednesday night church with them. Aunt May's Methodists didn't meet on Wednesdays, but Mrs. Jennings did. I thought a Methodist was a Methodist, so why drive twenty extra minutes to another Methodist church?

I asked about that. I discovered this was Mrs. Jennings' home church, and a twenty-minute ride was worth it to be reunited with sisters and their families every Wednesday night. The explanation made sense to me. I had sisters.

Everything Mrs. Jennings said seemed sensible. I admired her; she was a postmaster. Not many women held jobs in predominantly male positions or worked outside the home in the late '50s and '60s. Mrs. Jennings did. She was a role model for me. She was physically fit and would walk twenty miles a week on a trail that paralleled the

New River. Her personality was lovely and full of hope for all she met. She had three children, but she seemed my age at times yet very wise. I loved Ms. Jennings like I did my aunt May, and she was Dubs's mom. I couldn't find any fault with Dubs or Mrs. Jennings.

One night not long after the plank crime incident, the Plymouth pulled along the fence at the crab apple trees. I noticed only Mr. and Mrs. Jennings and Dubs were in it. Dubs, who was not a usual Wednesday night churchgoer, had come to get me to attend church to sit beside him. This had to be the reason for his presence. His older sister, Rachel Ann, and new baby sister, Sissy, were not in the car. Dubs Jennings got out like a gentleman and opened the door for me. This had not gone unnoticed by my uncle and aunt.

I got into the car, although my face felt hot for some reason. I suppose I was a little bit embarrassed in front of Aunt May and Uncle Art to be going on a bona fide "date," since Rachel Ann and Sissy were not coming to church with us. Two in the front and two in the back—like a double date but with parents.

The conversation was polite as the Jennings' asked about my family, school, and my uncle and aunt. I could tell Mrs. Jennings respected my aunt and enjoyed being the recipient of her good cooking at times.

I looked at Dubs several times on the twenty-minute sojourn. He was always looking at me, and he smiled that incredible heart-stopping smile. Mr. and Mrs. Jennings began talking about Mr. Jennings's job. This left Dubs and me to ourselves.

For only the second time since the "plank crime," Dubs mentioned Joe "Boney's" narrow escape through the plank hole on the bridge. We decided it was a relief that we had not been found out, and that good had come from bad since Joe "Boney" had profited by his overnight popularity from the situation.

We sat right there in the backseat of the Valiant Plymouth justifying our bad behavior. We agreed not to speak of it again and to forget pulling pranks. It was too risky, and we were too old. We laughed at our foolishness. I was assured Dubs did not have a criminal bone in his body, either.

With the plank crime behind us and our establishing how mature we were, Dubs seized the moment by scooting over and whispering, "Ducky, I have my driver's license now. Do you want to go to the drive-in movie Saturday night with me?"

Oh, brother, did I! "Yes, I do, Dubs, if Uncle Art and Aunt May will let me," I responded, flinging my most seductive smile, up to this point of my fifteen-year-old life.

During the church service, I sinned again. I failed to take in a single word the Methodist minister said. I was too preoccupied with plotting how I was going to get Uncle Art and Aunt May to let me go to the movies with Dubs Jennings.

Being a teenager was tough. I wanted to go with Dubs but was too embarrassed to ask. I needed to get over myself. I figured Aunt May would be the easier one to convince. I was counting on her skills as a fellow female to help me get permission from Uncle Art.

I was hoping he remembered young love, first dates, and life as a teenager. Well, on second thought, maybe I didn't.

Aunt May had found love, right? She had a daughter who married her first love. They had two sons who married. Aunt May knew about teenage girls, boys, and love. My bet would go on Aunt May to help me out. She just needed to think back to the time she was a young girl.

Uncle Art was a looker, as my mama had said. He had dark blue eyes and a dimple in the cleft of his chin. He was tall and nicely built for an older person, I guess you could say.

Aunt May was a rotund, short lady with serious brown eyes and brown hair, with just the slightest streaking of gray in her bangs. I thought she was as morally and spiritually good as any human I knew besides my mama and Mrs. Jennings. Her beauty to me was weighed by her endless kindness and boundless love for a middle child who was not her own. I would call my Aunt May a "platinum" person of exquisite human value who made the earth better by her mere presence.

Uncle Art must have seen these qualities in Aunt May, too. He was gentle with her and treated her respectfully. I knew I was my Aunt May's favorite of all her nieces and nephews. She made me feel unconditionally loved. She had to help me with my first car date with a boy, right?

Uncle Art must have found love, too. He married her. He surely knew how important it was for me to not turn down Dubs. Men knew that to get a "no" for a date was an ego deflator. After all, Uncle Art appeared to like Dubs. He cut his hair. He spoke or nodded to him from the porch when Dubs passed to get a look at me. He especially liked and respected his mother and father, so I felt this would be my "in" to Uncle Art saying "yes" to my going out with Dubs. Going without his parents along was the iffy thing about the situation, but I was counting on Aunt May to extol my good Methodist values and win him over to my side. Knowing the love and long marriage these two shared, I figured they would eventually agree to let their favorite niece, me, go with one of their favorite neighbor's boy, Dubs.

Aunt May and Uncle Art knew something about love. They had three children from their union. They surely dated or courted for a while, although they certainly didn't share any details of their past with me. If only they remembered that special feeling.

Nonetheless, I was depending on them both to let me go to the movies with Dubs.

On the way back to New River from the church service, Mr. and Mrs. Jennings talked about the minister's message. I hoped they would not ask me a thing about the message.

At this point I was so love-stricken, I barely could remember my name. I had not tuned in to the minister and would be unresponsive on the spiritual side at this time. All I was doing was thinking about the movie possibility with Dubs. They did not discuss the message and moved on to talking about seeing Mrs. Jennings's family. They left Dubs and me to talk between ourselves uninterrupted.

Darkness covered the New River like a cloak. The darkness seemed to make Dubs feel more comfortable, as he managed to slide closer to me. He took my hand just like he had at Hungry Mother State Park. This time he never turned my hand loose, not even when our hands became sweaty. Too quickly, we were about halfway to Uncle Art's house. How could holding a sweaty hand be so exciting? This love thing was just as confusing as it was enticing.

Something unexpected happened that night in the Plymouth Valiant. About halfway between the Fort Methodist Church trip and Aunt May's house, as I was in the middle of a conversation about Kate's Barracuda days, Dubs leaned gently over and brushed my lips with his.

He took my hand to his mouth and softly kissed the back of it. I was glad I had applied some of Aunt May's lavender lotion to it after my shower. I did my best at an awkward sideways kiss. My kissing experience was somewhat limited. I was picky and proud that I rationed my kisses and affection.

I had kissed the handsome lifeguard at Ms. Heaton's pool; I had kissed Greg Montgomery, the high school quarterback and random spinner of the bottle at Barb Broome's sixteenth birthday party; I had kissed my neighbor, Evan McGee, who taught me how to play the guitar, and Syd Perry at the corner of his house. But I had never been the recipient of a better, more lovely and meaningful kiss as Dubs gave. The tiny goose bumps that appeared on my arms signaled that this kiss was special.

I knew this was not only my first love but his as well. I remembered a few unclaimed lines in a poetry book, including "a kiss writes the secrets of the heart." He shared the secret within his heart with that kiss. He had reciprocated my feelings.

After arriving back to my summer haven, I left the Jennings' Valiant for the front porch. I sat down in Uncle Art's big rocker, closed my eyes, and imagined Dubs's kiss all over again. I hummed the few words of Elvis's "Moonlight Swim," through. "The air is cold with kisses oh, so sweet, I'll keep you warm oh, so very warm from head to feet," and thought the King of Rock must have been in love to have written those lyrics. Indeed, Dubs's kisses had warmed me from my head to my toes.

"Aunt May, Dubs Jennings asked me to go to the drive-in movie Saturday night. May I please go?"

I practiced those lines over and over in front of the mirror on the dresser, in the backyard under the mimosa branches, and in the shower.

No longer could I procrastinate; I had to ask today. It was Thursday, and I had to let Dubs know. I had to let me know.

After breakfast, I cleared the table, washed the dishes, poured extra hot water from the porcelain tea kettle over them, and visited Aunt May in her sewing room. I took my usual place on the daybed, took the button basket in my lap, and tried to conversationally warm up Aunt May.

"Aunt May, do you and Uncle Art ever go to the picture shows?"

"No," she answered flatly.

"Have you ever wanted to go to them?"

"No, Ducky, I haven't." So much for warming up Aunt May. She never missed a throttle on the Singer, intent on her neatly aligned stitches on a customer's pair of gray slacks.

Goodness, this was going to be harder than I thought. Aunt May was in a dour mood. I was going to have to rethink my strategy. Then, she finally kicked in on the last question. Nodding toward the barber shop, she retorted, "He wouldn't waste money on a picture show. Would you like to go to one, Ducky?"

Yes! She got the hint.

Now was my chance.

"I know how busy you are, and I know Uncle Art wouldn't want to waste his hard-earned money on a movie ticket for me, but Dubs ask me to go with him to the Wytheville picture show."

I held off on the drive-in part.

"He did, did he, Ducky?"

Now, what the Sam Hill was that question about?

"Yes, ma'am, and he will get my ticket, too. He gets to take his mom and dad's car, and he will bring me home when you say, and you can talk to Uncle Art about it to see if it is all right with him."

Aunt May retorted, "I will speak with Mrs. Jennings and him," as she nodded her head toward the barbershop and just kept on pumping the Singer metal foot pedal. She never missed a stitch. "Duck, I have to finish this dress for Mrs. Rosenbaum, so take my grocery list; go to Jenelle's for me."

I could tell she had to think about the answer. Calling me "Duck" told me to exit the conversation and the door. She had a timeline to keep.

She never gave me their answer until Friday after lunch. I never broached the subject again either, until she brought it up, although I was dying to ask. I was about to go to the front porch with Uncle Art when she summoned me to help her in the sewing room.

I walked behind her until she turned around and began, "Ducky, I have spoken with Mrs. Jennings and with him," nodding her head toward the front porch. "He is going to let you go, but you are to be home at 10:00 p.m., or he will not let you go again."

She continued, "Dubs hasn't been driving long, so I must ask you to not let him drive fast. If he does, and we find out, then you will never go again with him. Is that clear, Ducky?"

That part "will never get to go again" sounded promising for more time with Dubs, if he didn't speed or miss curfew. I would caution him on that, and I would wear a watch to keep alert. "Yes, Aunt May. I promise."

"Hey, Tony, this is Jessica from Tennessee," Dubs Jennings said. I had asked him to call me Jessica on the river bank several summers ago, but he was just now getting around to it. I could not see him introducing me as a "ducky" and I was thankful for that. He meant business. This was an official date without his parents. I felt official, too, with my given name, all grown up.

"Hi, Jessica, glad to meet you." Tony responded. "She's a looker, Dubs."

We seemed to be stopping by every place between the New River and Wytheville, places where Dubs's friends worked.

I was worrying about getting to the movie when Dubs grabbed my hand and pulled me toward him as the gray Valiant climbed the hill next to the Howard Johnson Motel.

We stopped in front of the motel. I almost hyperventilated, worrying about being seen at a Howard Johnson's when a dark-haired teen about Dubs's age appeared from the lobby.

Had Dubs Jennings phoned ahead to every friend he had?

"Hi, Edwin Wayne, is that the Tennessee girl you've been telling us about?"

"It sure is, Matt. This is Jessica Pearman."

I greeted Matt, as he practically crawled in the rolled-down glass on the driver's side to check me out. I was beginning to feel pretty good about myself. My blonde hair was shoulder length that summer. My royal blue ribbed knit sweater, borrowed from my Tennessee pool friend, Rosalind Jean Heaton, helped to show my new bust size. I had a matching A-line skirt from a store in Elizabethton, and I wore my new brown Wegian shoes.

This was pretty much the sum of my store-bought clothes for summer. I either had Aunt May's sewn ones, for which I was grateful, or hand-me-downs from Rose or Kate. I never was allowed to borrow clothing, but my friend Rosalind Jean let me take the sweater just in case I saw Dubs. I never told my mama I had it in my suitcase.

Jessie Shields Strickland

Rosalind was older and Grace Kelly-beautiful. She knew I needed that sweater for impact. She also knew what was in my measly wardrobe.

Dubs had remarked about my good looks the moment we were out of hearing distance from Uncle Art. That bolstered my ego considerably, and I thanked Rosalind silently. I returned his compliment by telling him he looked handsome. He wore a sand-colored sweater and chocolate-brown trousers.

We finally made it to the movie after it had started. Being late was fine since I really did not care what was playing—I was with Dubs. Dubs pulled into a spot . Being late, all the back of the lot was filled, and some of the car windshields were already fogged. Dubs rolled the driver's window down, hooked on the metallic speaker, adjusted it, and rolled the window back up.

Goldfinger with James Bond, starring Sean Connery, was in progress on the big outdoor screen. I was happy to my tiptoes.

Memories of such characters as "Pussy Galore" and "James Bond" were not the character types I would discuss with Aunt May or Uncle Art. I was sure of one thing: if I did, my dating days would be numbered. I was intrigued with the whole idea of this secret agent James Bond's life, but I just didn't know how to explain the plot or the characters.

Dubs must have gotten a jolt from the skimpy clothing, as he made a feeble attempt at groping my right breast when his hand "accidentally" fell in the precise vicinity of it after James Bond led the way on screen with Pussy Galore. Thanks, James Bond.

My face flushed as Dubs became more amorous. I exhausted myself trying to keep him at bay. I managed to do so. I knew without a doubt I loved Dubs, but I knew I would do nothing more than kiss. I had instilled in my soul my mama and Aunt May's expectations and morals. No matter how giddy or light headed I felt, I knew the limit to keep self respect. This time, unlike the bridge prank, it was not about being caught. No one was there to stop me. I got to make the decision of how far to go with a teenage boy at a drive-in picture show. I may have seemed a bit prudish to Dubs, but he continued to love me in return for my values. This was a lesson that was learned and lived by, and which got me many proposals of marriage.

As my mama said to my sisters and me when she gave us "the talk", no one really wants used goods. Naturally, she wanted to drive the point home so she conveyed the real-life stories of two wayward teen mothers in the community who had disgraced their families, ended up on government subsidy, dropped out of school, and never married. This was mama's sex-prevention strategy. It seemed to work on all four of us girls.

We drove the Valiant back to New River in time for curfew. All was well. *Even the more passionate kiss of my teenage friend hit the mark worthy of more girl talk when I went home to Tennessee,* I thought.

Dubs needed to stay away from James Bond movies, or he was headed for trouble. I, on the other hand, would not get to see another James Bond movie, since my mama monitored my whereabouts. That was okay. This one had been memorable, would last me, and had tested my

Methodist resolve. I felt I had passed a test with an "A". It felt good, and my restraint certainly did not cause any lack of affection on Dubs' part. He just seemed to like me that much more.

Dubs seemed different after the movie and in a good way. He didn't go fishing as much. He passed by Aunt May's house more often. He spent more time looking at me and lingered when one of us was summoned to come home before dark.

One afternoon, I walked to the porch to sweep it for Aunt May. I had no longer gotten the broom moving, when I saw Dubs descend in the family Plymouth down the hill. I immediately slowed my pace as to not finish the task too quickly or be too obvious in wanting to see him.

My heart was almost beating from my chest when the Plymouth began slowing down. I heard Dubs barely call my name. I turned my head in the direction of his hypnotizing voice and saw him mouth the three little words that every young girl in love wants to hear or see: *I love you.* His usual wink punctuated the mouthed words. I smiled so satisfyingly that I could have cracked my cheekbones.

That was it. As quickly as he appeared, he vanished along in the Plymouth toward Wytheville. That action endeared him even more to me, such bravery to do that so close to Uncle Art's barber shop.

He had seemed more disappointed than ever to see the summer come to a close. I knew we had become closer and more open with our feelings. I had even written a letter home to mama and the girls to tell them I had been asked to Dub's prom.

Dubs would be a senior at Fort Chatwell High School the following year. Before the summer ended, he asked me to come back as his date for the senior prom. He said he would send the details. I thought about Dubs, the drive-in, and the upcoming prom all the way back from the New River to Mama's house.

Kate had written me back to express her excitement that one of us had a real boyfriend and a life outside the mountain valley. I never thought she felt as strongly about leaving the River Doe as I, but, heck, she was an artist in training. She most definitely wanted to see the world and learn more about the master artists.

I was happy to hear from home, but that still did not make me want to arrive there anytime soon that fall. My thoughts were on Dubs and the prom. Being the lovestruck teens we were, we vowed to write each other, and we did several times throughout the fall and winter.

That invitation to the prom and Dubs mouthing the three words played through my mind many times as the Tennessee winter settled in on the Appalachian Mountains surrounding our clapboard river house.

In the spring, I wrote him to ask about the prom details. To my disappointment, he did not answer. I did not write him again. I was crushed.

I never mentioned the prom to my family after that because I would have shown my tremendous disappointment, and mama had enough to contend with without worrying about my feelings.

Oddly enough, my family did not mention Dubs or the prom to me, even though, I had written them in the summer. We had talked for hours about my feelings for Dubs when I had returned that summer. This was not ordinary behavior for me or them. Until that fall, I kept most of my amorous feelings about Dubs treasured in my heart and only pulled them out in the sweetest of my dreams.

"Sher…r…y baby, won't you be my girl?" blasted from the jukebox at Gurney's onto the surrounding campus of the high school my sisters and I attended in the fall of that year. We were going to an old brick high school at Hampton, which was due for demolition. The mountain kids had overtaken the hallways and classrooms. Change was a must, and a new high school was in progress about three miles up the road toward Roan Mountain. The greatest reward for the overcrowding of Hampton High School was the old cafeteria would not hold us, and the Gurney Burger Hut across the state highway was ours for the walking. Walking across the State Highway 67 to the Gurney Burger Hut was a Hampton hallmark treasured by all who traversed it.

    The seniors had control of the best booths. Vitalis and ducktails, a haircut which required a substantial amount of store-ought hair oil to be combed in longer hair from front to back in the shape of a duck's tail feathers which only the cool guys wore, identified the senior boys. The girls' hairstyles were sprayed with Aqua Net and teased to create the perfect beehive or rounded bell shape. We loved to listen to Otis Redding's "Under the Boardwalk", and eat our favorite food, a mouth-watering Gurney burger was made from a large, hand-kneaded pound of ground round beef, a secret ingredient, salt and peppered just right, slathered with mayo, ketchup, lettuce and slid between a gigantic, sesame seed bun that had been warmed.

If we had saved our money, several of us split the burger in equal chunks and even ordered a basket of crispy, browned French fries to divide. No one ordered onions for their burgers or dogs—this was the kiss of dateless death.

Most shared from someone's plate of food. No one left hungry. Mountain kids looked after each other even if it was the sharing of the best burger ever. If we pooled our money, we could get a soft drink, a "pop," with multiple straws. I always took the first sip. *No way,* I thought, *should I sip a pop after someone else sipped from the same bottle.* The others indulged me. They knew this was where I drew the line in sharing. The only thing missing from this idyllic teenage time was Dubs. Even though he had failed to respond to my last letter, I had not been successful in erasing him from my memory.

The school year passed swiftly. I did well in my studies, as did my sisters Kate and Helen. Boys had begun taking serious interest in us, much to our mama's chagrin. I had crushes and dates but never thought past Dubs Jennings for a serious boyfriend myself except for one Tennessee boyfriend, Rhett Harmon. He was my mama's favorite male for me to date. He was kind, honest, hard-working, nice-looking, athletic, protective, and loved me—what was not to like? The problem was and would be young hormonal girls just see their mother's wisdom sometimes too late. No matter how hard I tried, I expected to feel the same butterfly stomachs and skipping heart palpitations I had with Dubs.

Kate was accepting dates but would seem to disappear when they came for her. Mama would make excuses and try to force Helen or me to fill in for Kate. I was reluctant and held my ground. Poor Helen substituted for Kate a couple of times only to be miserable and swear never to be Kate's dating sub again. The odd thing was the boys seemed perfectly happy with this arrangement. One of the Pearman girls was better than no Pearman girl, especially with the 25-cents-a-gallon for gas the boys had to spend to get to our river house.

We concluded Kate was socially challenged when it came to the opposite sex. She preferred getting absorbed in her literary and art studies. Italy and France along with Picasso and Michelangelo were her loves. The mountains stifled her creativity. She escaped into this world after we went to bed. Many times upon waking, Mama would find Kate's slumbering body across the foot of the bed and one of her "masterpieces" in French Impressionism still drying on the old vanilla-colored easel, or a Walt Whitman book opened facedown across her chest. Kate always beat to a different drum-—a perfectly good drum, far ahead intellectually of our understanding.

She was never able to be herself in a mountain settlement, culturally limited to a drive-in picture show . Mama had arranged for her to be taken to Johnson City and to study art with John Maxwell, who was a capable mentor, and Edgar Bowlin, a travelling artist making a stop through Elizabethton who had painted President Eisenhower. These were favorite times for Kate. She never lost her love of art.

Back and forth, back and forth, I walked to the faded gray mailbox beside the old dirt road unless Mama or Helen beat me to it. Kate never cared what was in the mailbox and didn't waste her energy or take time from reading or drawing.

I never did hear from Dubs Jennings about the details of the senior prom, and time was getting short, with only a couple of weeks until school would be out for the summer. Every day that I found that mailbox empty, I became more disappointed in a teenage boy named Dubs who had given his word to a girl who had exposed her heart unselfishly to him.

I finally quit asking, "Mama, did I get a letter today?" She would look at me with the saddest eyes and shake her head no. I looked for that letter all my junior year to no avail.

For the first summer since early childhood, I did not stay with Aunt May and Uncle Art in Austinville along the New River. I wrote to Aunt May, Uncle Art, and Uncle Emmett to tell them. I simply was not up to it.

To see Dubs Jennings after he had broken his word and had obviously betrayed me was too hard to take. I wanted to forget this godlike boy I had built up in my mind over ten summers.

The prom had long passed. My affection for Dubs had not. For the first time in my life, I tasted rejection. It stung worse than a wasp. Rejection was not my friend.

My mama said, "Time will heal," yet I must have been slower in the healing process than most. I felt the hurt for years to come. A promise was made and not kept. I would find it a slow process to trust and love again. I had not learned why he did not write to me. I had too much pride to ever ask or write to him again.

I made the most of my summer. Kate had matriculated. Now, she could enjoy all the art and literature she wanted. She thrived among those of her kind. I believe this was the happiest we had ever seem Kate, other than the day she got the 1966 navy Barracuda .

Helen was a sophomore in high school, and I would be a senior. We had moved into the new high school. It was the newest building within fifty miles of our home. Helen and I thrived there. We loved being in the same school together. She was my little sister by two years, and she was my best friend.

We were elected cheerleaders and beauty pinups representing our classes. Rhett, the captain of the football team, had his own car and asked me to the movies many times. He liked me.

I preferred the walk-in theater to the drive-in movie. I had too many memories of Dubs Nuchols at the drive-in, baseball games, picnics, and state park outings. I made every effort to make new memories with the football captain. I found it difficult.

Senior year came to a successful closure for me. I, too, would be attending college, but I would start the summer term rather than wait for fall.

Again, I did not travel to New River for summer, although I did get to see Aunt May and Uncle Art when they came to the late summer family reunion in Tennessee. It was a Pearman pack roundup with about thirty families and cousins we had not seen in years.

My aunt Wilson and my aunt Miranda organized the event at a park in the Great Smokey Mountains. Food variety of the Southern style, black bear sightings, welcoming new family faces, reminiscing about the dearly departed, and "catching up" on the old folks made the reunion just that—a reunion!

I sure was glad to see Aunt May's good cooking had stayed true to form.

There was no mention of Dubs until Aunt May was about to leave for the trip back to the New River.

She looked at me, "Ducky, did you know Dubs is at college studying to be an architect?"

No, I didn't, but any news of Dubs was good news. I just could not forget him.

I was dying to inquire for more information but wanted to be nonchalant about my feelings, so I just shook my head no. I wanted to cry as all the feelings I thought to hide away came rushing back like the River Doe when she floods her banks.

Aunt May was in tune with my thoughts, hugged me hard, and kissed my cheek.

I committed right then and there to myself to finish college, just like Mama did, Rose did, and Kate and Helen would do. Even if my mama was short on cash, she was never short on high expectations, so this would please her and help me forget Dubs finally.

College life was agreeable. Kate and I had a few classes together. This always confused the professors. Kate insisted I take art history with her. She had the edge. She enjoyed her newfound confidence and started to date a musician. I had some interest in art history but none in the musician. Kate would soon learn about a broken heart and a broken promise, too. My heart ached for her. She never fully recovered from it.

In my junior year, I decided to major in English, and Helen was a freshman majoring in elementary education. Kate, Helen, and I took a history course together with the same professor. He called us the "three sisters." That stuck with us until the last one of us graduated. "Hey, sisters!" was often heard when we would be walking about campus, in restaurants, or shopping. We knew someone knew at least one of us if not all three of us.

Helen and Kate would become excellent teachers, and Helen was always the lucky one at love. Other than the death of our father and brother, Helen had an almost painless life. She chose her profession and her husband wisely. Love begat love with baby sister Helen. My heart runneth over with love for her, as she was the youngest of my mama's five children and was always called the baby of the family even into adulthood.

My mama encouraged me to date her favorite "pick" for me, Rhett. I did.

I tried to move on after discovering Rhett loved me as much as I did Dubs. I had turned selfish. I never revealed my feelings about Dubs to Rhett. In the long run, I should have, because I ended up breaking Rhett's heart just as my heart had been broken.

Rhett and I dated throughout the last two years of high school through college. I loved Rhett because he was kind, generous, handsome, and dependable. My mother trusted him with me.

In my freshman college year, Rhett was drafted into the army. I did not see him very much after that unless he was on military leave, and that depended where he was stationed. We wrote to each other frequently. He had professed his love to me and given me a beautiful diamond ring my junior year in college. Within a week after the engagement, he was sent to Germany with his next military assignment. While he was in Germany, I refuted the adage absence makes the heart grow fonder. For me, it did not.

My mother was beside herself with the engagement. I had taken his diamond ring because I thought I had loved Rhett enough; only during his absence I realized it was like the love for a best friend. After all, he was the first boy I dated more than a few dates after my brother was killed in the airline crash. He was there for my family at that tragic time. His kindness was beyond measure to me, my mama, and sisters. He ran errands, talked with my mama for hours to help lighten her thoughts about the loss of Howard, and took my sisters with us to ballgames or the Gurney Burger Hut.

Mama was right on every count about Rhett. He would have made a wonderful husband, but I knew it would not be to me. The longer he was away, the more I knew I could not marry Rhett. He deserved to be loved and the receiver of more passion than I could give. As hard as I tried, I could not seem to feel the emotions I had felt for Dubs. I looked for the giddiness, lightheadedness, butterfly stomach, goose bumps, or that something that spoke to my senses; unfortunately, I did not find it.

My senior year in college while Rhett was still in Germany, I took the coward's way out and much to my mama's chagrin, I broke the engagement. I could not marry Rhett. I loved Rhett enough to know he was a fine young man who needed a marriage partner who would cherish his goodness and shower him with love and passion. Rhett deserved this. This was a character flaw in me I never repeated.

To hurt someone who had been kind and loving to me was the most cruel. My mama was sincerely hurt and disappointed in me for treating this fine young man who adored me so badly. The day Rhett returned from Germany, he came to see my mama, then me. I saw the hurt in his face, but even then, he showed such strength of character. He never spoke loudly or disrespectfully. He was the kind, considerate Rhett. He was the type person that every mama wants for her daughter.

I returned his ring; he hugged me, and he left only returning when I was not at home to see my mama. He did not stay in our community but moved to Michigan. He continued to return for visits with mama even after he married. My mama told me about each visit. She was the most excited when he brought his young daughter to see her. Distance did not matter to Rhett. He followed this same pattern even after his own parents and brother died. He visited my mama for thirty-five years until her death.

I finally saw Rhett two years ago at my sister Kate's funeral. Many years had passed since handing him the diamond back when I was nineteen years old. He looked quite the same; he had kept his beautiful smile, dark thick hair, and his physically fit body. I, on the other hand, was heavier. The cheerleader figure was long gone, as was the long blonde hair.

Rhett did not seem to mind. He had forgiven me in the lovely, peaceful, and kind manner I knew so well. His embrace wiped away years of sadness and guilt for me which I had carried. Odd how a death can be healing. My sister Kate loved Rhett, too, as my mother had. They would have been pleased to know our paths crossed, and Kate had a hand in it.

"Ducky, are you going with us?" Mama asked.

"Yes, I am going. I want to see Uncle Art and Aunt May." I was looking forward to the trip to Austinville and the New River with Mama, Kate, and Helen. It had been four years. I was excited and at the same time anxious.

My love for Aunt May and Uncle Art was more pronounced than that of my anxiety. I had completely lost track of Dubs, except that reasoning told me he would be a senior in college.

We had no sooner than gotten to the New River and into Aunt May's house when she whispered in my ear,

"Ducky, you should know Edwin Wayne is getting married next weekend. I'd rather you hear that from me first than Sue Ann or Mrs. Jennings."

I had been healing four years, as I believed time had helped. However, those words made me feel nauseated and sad to my bones.

I changed the subject, "Where is Uncle Art today?" I had no sooner gotten the question out of my mouth when a knock at the door came.

Aunt May said, "Who in the world could that be? He (nodding her head toward the barbershop) never knocks." She opened the door, and there, standing with only a storm door separating us, was none other than Dubs.

Ten wide eyes were upon him. Mine surely were the widest. Dubs confidently greeted Aunt May, Mama, Helen, and Kate, and then asked, "Jessica, can I speak with you outside?"

Leaving my aunt, mama, and sisters speechless, I went with Dubs out the door. As from the past, Dubs caught my hand and took me to the driveway where a motorcycle was parked. Without saying a word, I climbed on the back. As we left the drive, I looked toward the barbershop to see Uncle Art with a handkerchief, wiping his eyes.

Dubs changed gears, and as we traveled toward Wytheville, I wrapped my arms around him closely, as I was unaccustomed to being on a motorcycle.

"Do you know how glad I am to see you, Ducky?" he said after angling his head toward me.

I was speechless.

He continued, "I want to take you to a special place. We can talk then."

That is precisely what we did. We left the bike and walked to an overlook of the New River near Wytheville.

As we walked together, he would look over and smile—the mesmerizing smile from the riverbank, the dock at Hungry Mother Park, church, the drive-in, and after the stolen kiss.

Dubs was the Dubs I had known and loved, and only a step away. The array of multicolored leaves had started to fall from the branches that had secured them. A rumbling was heard from the New River as it slapped against rocks and riverbank along its pathway.

"Ducky, oh, Ducky." He pulled me around to face him and kissed my forehead, each cheek, my chin, and the tops of my hands, and then the warmth of his lips covered mine.

We were in the moment. All was forgiven. But doubt remained.

"Dubs, how can you do this? Aunt May said you are getting married next weekend."

"Ducky, I love you. I have always loved you. You love me, don't you?"

"Yes, I love you and think I have since I was ten, but you are marrying someone next week?"

"But I only love you, Ducky. I want to marry you. Will you go away with me, marry me, Ducky?"

I could not separate the E.W. "Dubs" Jennings I was hearing from the young teenager by the same name who had broken his word and my heart with it.

"Dubs, who is the girl you are supposed to marry next week?"

"Ducky, do you remember when you did not answer my letter about coming back to Fort Chatwell for my prom? Junior's cousin went with me at the last moment. Do you remember Junior?" (I did remember Junior, that no-good Dodger who had set Dubs up with the prom date cousin that was leading to his marriage. How could I ever forget Junior?) "I have dated her ever since."

"Ducky, I thought you had found someone else and didn't like me anymore. I wrote you several letters, but you never answered me."

I was hurt. How could he say this? I checked the mailbox every day, or at least Mama, Helen, or I had. How could he turn on and off such feelings? He was being untruthful.

"Will you leave with me, Ducky? If you will, I will call off the wedding. I want you, not her."

My heart yearned to say yes. Mama's high expectations screamed. *No, I can't. I have only two quarters before I graduate college. Dubs, you broke a promise before. How can I believe you now?*

Kate's musician had hurt her enough to last a lifetime, so I stepped back, looked at Dubs, and said, "E.W., I love you, but I can't marry you."

I can remember crying when I said it. I believed he had never written to me about the prom. I remembered how many years I had tried to forget him. I could not take another heart break. I did not want to be hurt like Kate had been hurt. We held on to each other for as long as we could stand there on the knoll by the New River.

Jessie Shields Strickland

I have thought many times about how that came out and regretted not adding "now." I gave him no hope. Why could I have not told him how I really felt about believing that I not received a letter? I could have asked him to wait for me to graduate in a half year, and if he had truly loved me, he would have. I closed it with finality because of my pride and Mama's expectations. The words were spoken insincerely. They were empty words.

I loved Dubs. I could never seem to love as deeply as I had loved him; he was my first love, with all the youthful happiness of ten innocent and carefree summers.

He kissed me again. We looked each other in the eyes, revealing sadness to both our young souls. We gave one final embrace. We got on the bike and left, veiled in quietness and ignorant to the roar of the cycle and traffic. Our lives would not follow a parallel course, intersected.

He took me to Aunt May's door and never looked me in my eyes. He squeezed my hands and left the porch where I had sat with Uncle Art for hours smelling crab apple blossom scent with thoughts of Dubs Jennings and hoping for a glimpse of him on the hill.

He took equal parts of my heart and youth with him from the front porch that day.

Helen opened the door for me to come in before I could turn the knob. "Oh, shucks," Kate said. "I hoped you would elope while you were out." Weak laughter permeated the room. Kate meant it. The others had hoped it. I wished it.

We visited with Aunt May and Uncle Art for a while longer. Appetites were lost, even though Aunt May tried her best. I passed on the hot ham shank biscuits. This was a dead giveaway that I was suffering to all those around the bountifully spread table who knew my voracious appetite.

The time came for us to leave. I got several extra-long farewell hugs from Aunt May and Uncle Art, who had even closed the barbershop earlier than usual to see us off. My aunt and uncle had wanted this to turn out differently. They had felt a part of the romance. I left them sad and disappointed not for them, but for me.

I never looked to the top of the hill for fear of seeing of the Jennings's house. My heart and I had enough for one day. Leaving on this day made my future return trips to Aunt May's and Uncle Art's home oddly different. One takes for granted the uniqueness of total joy when one is experiencing it. Lasting joy, first love, and carefree youth are elusive.

Mama came up with an idea to visit Cousin Florence's over at Cripple Creek. She said we would do a quick visit and then start for Tennessee. She hoped my cousin Sam would be home, since he was my favorite cousin and could break a blue mood quickly with his dry humor and Cripple Creek tales of mischief.

Cripple Creek had once been a thriving mining town in southwestern Virginia. My mama knew everyone there. Seldom did people her age move away. They had set down roots and were buried there.

We were nearing Cripple Creek when Mama looked over at me. I was driving. Tears started tumbling down her cheeks.

"Duck, pull over." She had gotten our full attention. Helen and Kate were in the backseat hanging on every word.

I did as she requested. I could tell she was becoming emotionally distraught. Other than the death of my father, my brother, and during the Hans Christian Anderson's story, *The Little Match Girl,* she told us at Christmas, I had never seen her cry.

"Mama, what's wrong?" I asked.

"Ducky, I have ruined your life. I will never forgive myself, and I don't think you will ever forgive me for what I have done."

"Mama," I said, "what have you ever done to hurt me or any of us that would make you say something like that?"

My mama put her head into the palms of her hands, and sobbed pitifully.

She had our full attention. My sisters and I heard her utter the unbelievable, "Ducky, E.W. Jennings did keep his promise. He did write to you. I got those letters, read them, and burned them."

Helen cried out first, "Oh, no, Mama. Why?"

Kate questioned, "Mother, you surely would not do Ducky like that, would you?"

Mama went on, "Yes, I am ashamed to say I did do that. I could not see how I could afford to get her to Austinville and buy nice clothes for her to wear, so I destroyed the letters. It never occurred to me how much she liked him until today. Your Aunt May said she knew I had done something because his mother had asked her why Ducky didn't write back. Mrs. Jennings told May Dubs was hurt.

He waited to the last minute to ask Junior's cousin. The girl he is marrying now."

"He does love you, Ducky. I think I have ruined your life, his life, and my life by keeping this from you. I was wrong. At the time, it seemed the right thing to do. Now, I don't think so. Can you ever find it in your heart to forgive me, child?"

It was out. Mama could not bear it any longer.

Right there alongside the weedy, dandelion-filled country roadside from Austinville to Cripple Creek, we all started bawling. Mama, Helen, Kate, and me—our hearts were in sync to sadness and lost love, and what could have been. It was not Dubs who had betrayed me; it was Mama. The last person in the world that I thought would have hurt me, did. I saw the painful remorse cloaking her face and the forgiveness she sought in her damp eyes.

We arrived heartbroken to our Cripple Creek cousins' home. Cousin Sam tried his best to provide a good time. He took my sisters and me on a walk up the hillside to the mud dam. He joked all the way there and back. I knew why he was my favorite cousin. He could make me laugh. I needed a good laugh because thirty minutes earlier I did not think I would laugh again.

Cousin Florence made us feel welcome. She never questioned the sniffles or red eyes we had on arrival. I was sure that while my sisters and I were with Cousin Sam, Mama was spilling the beans of our personal business to Cousin Florence. Mama needed someone to talk with, and Cousin Florence was the perfect confidante. The stop at Cripple Creek made a nice diversion from my heartache and mama's regrets.

We started the long drive home to the River Doe. If we got too tired, we knew we could stop for the night in Marion, Virginia. Mama said it was up to us. She was trying her hardest to bring a little joy back inside Kate's silver blue Chevy II.

We rode the 102 miles in polite silence. We were all glad to be back to our Tennessee home. This night familiarity did breed contentment as well as exhaustion.

Mama never seemed to forgive herself. She would sometimes mention my unrequited love, but I never spoke of it. I had to forget the past. Move on. She had faith that I could do that. I stung for years from the pain of it. I knew she had done what she felt was her only choice at the time. I tried to bury that hurt and disappointment. To me, she was still the salt of the earth. I did forgive her. I told her many times when she asked me over the years.

My mama gave her whole life to her children and grandchildren. Her thoughts had been on getting a college degree for each of us. Finding a suitable husband was not to interfere with that. Even though Rose married young, she still finished college. Her education had spared us from being in the poorhouse. Most women in the majority of the twentieth century depended on a man for the family's living. My mama had been an exception to that. She was well educated and knew how to handle the family business. It was difficult with the absence of our daddy, but it was not financially devastating. She was afraid that if one of us lost our husband, that person needed to be educated to take care of self and family. We also had a couple of unmarried aunts who got along beautifully without a man in their lives. They were well educated, independent, and childless. Mama was an avid believer that education was the great equalizer for humanity. Her belief became a gift and a blessing to us.

I could find another love, perhaps, but never a better mother. Forgiveness made me whole and was the only course of action.

I placed my long-stemmed red rose on the coffin, and the first shovelfuls of dirt were cast over Aunt May's remains. I knew where she would sleep and that would be beside Uncle Art tonight. With a bundle of memories and a pocket full of sadness, I carefully walked along the rows of granite and marble markers toward my car with my family. Mama was right. I had learned to love again. Aunt May and Uncle Art would have approved. Kindness, honesty, hard work, compassion, and love were some of the many gifts Aunt Mary and Uncle Art had so genuinely and generously bestowed on me. My New River summers had been the very best part of my growing up.

After all, my Aunt May gave me a magical retreat where I explored very personal, first-time emotions. I will never forget the New River summers, and the friends I made there.

First love is not quite like anything I have experienced. It was a measuring device for me to gauge my boyfriends by. I may have passed on some great husband catches, but

I did finally feel those first love feelings with my husband Hamilton, whom I have affectionately called "Milt" for thirty-four years. He measured up, so I married him. He had the best of the Dubs and the Rhetts of the world. I needed those experiences to know what to seek in a marriage partner.

My wish is for every girl to have this almost mystical time in her life of knowing a first love. Going from a childish way of viewing the opposite sex in the world to a new dimension that exposes one's deepest emotions is incomparable to anything else. A first love seems to top all relationships that follow on the emotional barometer: the innocence and honesty of it, the butterfly stomach, giddy laughter, and secret thoughts kept in the heart for another.

After sixty-two years, I find myself occasionally thinking about Dubs Jennings. Age or marital status never truly vanishes one's feeling of love that is deep rooted. I don't feel embarrassed or ashamed of those feelings, because they were grown from an innocent time in life unscathed by a former emotion of this kind.

Dubs appears in my thoughts as the handsome, muscular, sandy-haired teenager on the New River bank. He is always leaned against the formidable trunk of the tree, where a brilliant Virginia sun streaked rays of light to create an unforgettable, perfect image for a teenage girl called Ducky. What if? Ah, a girl can dream, can't she?